12-7

From the "People Are Talking" Column of the *Eastwick, Connecticut Gazette*

Scandal lurks around every corner!

Who is that dashing man who's been spotted hanging around Eastwick ever since heiress Mary Duvall waltzed back into town? Could it be *that* Kane Brentwood—the divorced English lord who once had a thing for the beautiful black sheep of the Duvall clan? Rumor has it the two once had an illicit *arrangement,* but everything came crashing down when he married a woman more suitable for British high society.

Now that he's single again, could he be hoping to revive their involvement? He sure looks like the kind of man who'll stop at nothing to lure Ms. Duvall back into his bed. But Ms. Duvall had best be careful. One whiff of scandal and all her millions could go up in smoke....

Dear Reader,

Scandals, secrets and a very sexy man from her past are all a part of this new life that Mary Duvall is carving out for herself. Since I married my sweetheart when I was twenty-one, there's not much scandal lingering in my past, but I loved the fact that Mary's life abounds with it.

Her hero, Kane Brentwood, is a British gentleman who has never doubted that the one thing he wants in his life is Mary, whether as his mistress or as his wife. In my mind Kane is a mix between the devastatingly handsome Hugh Grant and the supersexy Clive Owen. Kane has all of Hugh's urban suavity and Clive's arrogant determination to win the woman he loves at all costs—like he did in the movie *Closer*—especially since Kane mirrors the same determination when it comes to Mary.

Enjoy!

Katherine

KATHERINE GARBERA

THE ONCE-A-MISTRESS WIFE

Silhouette
Desire

Published by Silhouette Books
America's Publisher of Contemporary Romance

Special thanks and acknowledgment are given to Katherine Garbera for her contribution to the SECRET LIVES OF SOCIETY WIVES miniseries.

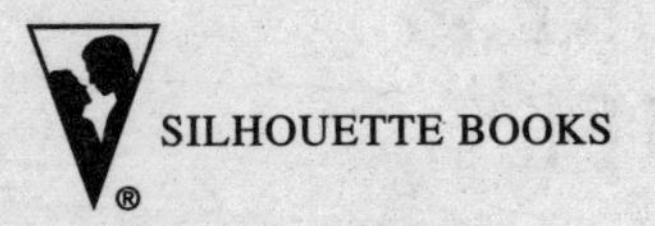

ISBN-13: 978-0-373-76749-6
ISBN-10: 0-373-76749-8

THE ONCE-A-MISTRESS WIFE

This edition published by arrangement with Harlequin Books S.A.

Visit Silhouette Books at www.eHarlequin.com

Printed in U.S.A.

Recent books by Katherine Garbera

Silhouette Desire

In Bed with Beauty #1535
Cinderella's Christmas Affair #1546
Let It Ride #1558
Sin City Wedding #1567
Mistress Minded #1587
Rock Me All Night #1672
†*His Wedding-Night Wager* #1708
†*Her High-Stakes Affair* #1714
†*Their Million-Dollar Night* #1720
The Once-A-Mistress Wife #1749

Silhouette Bombshell

Exposed #10
Night Life #23
The Amazon Strain #43
Exclusive #94

*King of Hearts
†What Happens in Vegas…

KATHERINE GARBERA

is the award-winning, bestselling author of more than twenty books for Silhouette and has been nominated for *Romantic Times BOOKclub*'s Career Achievement Awards in Series Fantasy and Series Adventure. Katherine recently moved to the Dallas area, where she lives with her husband and their two children. Visit Katherine on the Web at www.katherinegarbera.com.

This book is dedicated to the ladies of Nation Drive—
Kim, Michele and Kathy—who've made me feel
welcome and at home in Texas.

Acknowledgments:

Thanks to the other Society Wives ladies
who made working on this book such a pleasure...
Maureen, Metsy, Pat, Alison and Bronwyn.

Also a special thanks to Wanda Ottewell and
Melissa Jeglinski, for asking me to participate
in this fun series!

One

Mary Duvall stood over the open casket of her grandfather, David Duvall. Tears burned the back of her eyes, but she kept them in check, very conscious that Grandfather David had always wanted her to be composed in public. That's why she'd closed the doors to the viewing room and entered it alone.

The old Mary would have wept loudly and cried her grief with sobs and moans, doing everything in her power to get those emotions out. But now she buttoned them down. Ignored everything but the need to touch his face one last time.

She touched his cold, makeup-covered skin and shivered inside. She felt so alone. She *was* all alone now. Her parents had died years ago in a car accident—not that they'd ever been close. And her younger brother, their perfect child, had been in the car with them—also gone.

She liked the new life she was carving for herself in Eastwick, Connecticut, at her grandfather's behest. She'd returned from Paris when she'd learned his health was failing. He'd offered to make her his heir if she proved she was no longer the rebellious wild child he remembered.

"I'm going to make you proud, Grandfather. No more embarrassment over my behavior."

She leaned down, brushing her lips over his dry forehead and wishing for just one second that he could embrace her. Her childhood had been difficult to say the least and Grandfather David had been as disapproving as everyone else in the Duvall clan, but he'd always hugged her as she left.

He was the only one to ever do anything like that. She would miss him more than she'd realized.

A knock on the door interrupted her farewell.

She glanced at her watch. Damn, it was almost time for the public viewing. No doubt her cousins would be outside demanding some private time with a man they cared about only for his money.

Mary wanted to use the Duvall estate to benefit others. She intended to establish a trust that would be used to create neonatal units at hospitals in lower-income areas. She also hoped to sponsor an art-focused summer camp for underprivileged children. She had never been encouraged to paint as a child, even though her earliest memories were of having a paintbrush in her hand. She loved to create new worlds on canvas.

Her work was garnering attention in Europe and she enjoyed the money she'd made selling the serial rights to several of her pieces for a print series.

But for now, she had the viewing to get through. Before opening the door, she tucked the short note she'd written last night into the breast pocket of his suit, under his handkerchief, right over his heart.

Then she wiped the moisture from beneath her eyes and confronted her second cousins. Channing and Lorette Moorehead were the children of her grandfather's sister.

"How touching. I almost believe you cared for the old man," Channing said, escorting his sister Lorette to the casket.

"I did care for him," Mary said.

"Then why did you spend so many years breaking his heart?" Lorette asked.

Mary swallowed hard, biting back a retort that wouldn't be ladylike. Wouldn't fit the image that Grandfather wanted her to portray.

"We made our peace, Grandfather and I."

"You may have fooled Uncle David, but we aren't convinced you've changed. I will be keeping an eye on you," Channing said.

He was almost ten years older than she was, and from her earliest memories he'd always been a pompous ass. She had no fondness for Channing, but Lorette, who was only two years older than Mary, had been a close friend when they were younger. They'd roamed all over Grandfather's mansion playing games and getting into trouble. It had all ended when Lorette had turned ten and declared herself too old for childish pursuits.

"I'll leave you two to your private grieving."

The anteroom was almost empty except for a few of her friends. Their long history and regular luncheons had garnered them the name the Debs Club.

Everyone in their group seemed to be getting engaged or married; something Mary had no desire to do herself. She'd been deeply in love with a man once, and when he'd left her to marry the "right" kind of woman, she'd promised herself she'd never live with that kind of pain again.

Yet another example of how her wild lifestyle—which wasn't really that wild—had resulted in her being alone. The problem was that for most of her life Mary had never wanted to follow the rules. Almost in contradiction to the plain name—and possibly plain aspirations—her parents had given her at birth, Mary had come out of the womb a rebel.

But not any longer. She'd paid a high price for her rebelliousness, and her deathbed promise to Grandfather David meant she'd toe the line from now on.

Mary started toward her friends. They all wore black for mourning, and Mary appreciated having them here. Maybe she wasn't completely alone. She did have her friends, and they'd proven to be a solid support to her in a way that she'd never experienced before.

The outer door opened before she reached her friends, and she turned to greet the newcomer. The blood rushed to her head and she heard the pounding of her own heartbeat in her ears as she recognized the one man she'd never thought to see again.

Kane Brentwood—English lord and her ex-lover.

"Kane?"

"Mary," he said. Just her name in that deep voice of his never failed to send shivers coursing through her body.

She couldn't face him now. Not today, when she was struggling to keep her composure carefully in place. Not when she was so close to losing it.

At the sight of him, she was overwhelmed with the weight of the secrets between them. Secrets that, if revealed, would cost her everything—Grandfather's inheritance, Kane's respect and her own hard-won peace.

She tried to regain her composure, but she saw stars dancing in front of her eyes as he approached her. And then everything went black.

Kane Brentwood caught Mary just before she hit the floor. He was aware of the murmuring of voices behind him, but he didn't pay attention to anyone save the woman in his arms. His woman. She hadn't been taking very good care of herself. She'd lost weight and her skin was pale. He wondered if she'd mended bridges with her grandfather and what that had cost her.

He cupped her face. "Mary."

Her eyes blinked open, and he stared into that familiar Caribbean-blue color, reminding him of the month they'd spent at his vacation home in the British Virgin Islands. "Mary-Belle, are you okay?"

"Kane?"

"Yes, darling."

As she looked up at him, confusion knitted her brow. "I'm not your darling anymore."

A spear of anger went through him and he had to tamp down on his instinctive response, which was to take her in his arms and prove that she was still his. To prove that Mary would react to him the way she had from the first moment they met. But she was a married woman now, and he knew the way she felt about married people and affairs.

"We can discuss that later," he said.

A spark lit her eyes, the kind that in the past had always led to a spirited argument and then eventually to the bedroom. "Will your wife take part in the discussion?"

"I'm divorced. And your husband?"

She flushed and shook her head. "No husband."

No husband. She was free. He felt a surge of possessive determination. Now that he had her back in his arms, he wasn't going to let her go again. He'd done his bit for family and lineage, and that had cost him—more than he ever wanted this woman to know. They were both available again, and he was suddenly determined not to screw up the way he had before. He would not lose her again.

"Mary? Are you okay?"

He glanced over his shoulder to see four women walking toward him with a group of men a few steps behind. He tightened his hold on Mary.

"I'm fine, Emma. I didn't sleep well last night."

He wondered how much of that was due to her child. He didn't know much about the little blighters, but every book he'd read had said that they were time-consuming.

There were dark circles under her eyes, and he wished for a moment he still had the right to carry her out of this room, to find a private place. But he didn't. He lowered her to the ground, deliberately torturing himself by allowing her body to rub against his.

There were too many people around to have the discussion they needed to have. And he wanted—no, needed—to simply hold this woman who looked too fragile.

She took a step away from him, but he held onto her wrist.

"What are you doing?" she asked.

"Claiming what is mine," he said, stating the truth of why he was in Eastwick, especially now that he knew there was no husband. When he'd first read the announcement of David Duvall's death in the *Wall Street Journal,* he'd barely taken note of the fact—until he'd seen Mary's name listed as next of kin.

He'd been quietly searching for her for over a year now. His men hadn't been able to find any trace of her at the Paris apartment building where he'd last known her to live.

"I'm not yours anymore," she said again, tugging hard and pulling her hand away from him.

"Come with me," he said.

"Why?"

"I want to speak to you," he said, ignoring her friends.

"We are speaking, Mr. Brentwood."

"Alone," he said, using his hold on her waist to draw her closer to him. She had always had the ability to make him forget all rules of good breeding and react like a man. He felt the urge to do something horribly crass, such as toss her over his shoulder and carry her out of this room.

"I don't think that's a good idea."

He should never have put her on her feet. He should have kept her in his arms…where she belonged. "Don't push me, Mary-Belle. I'm not in the mood for it."

She stiffened at the nickname and gave him a hard

glare. He lowered his head, brushing his lips against hers. A surge of arousal shot through his body as her mouth opened under his—the same way it always had. He slipped his tongue between her lips, hungry for her taste. It had been too damned long since he'd sated himself on Mary.

Someone cleared their throat, and Mary pulled away from him. Kane kept his hand on her waist and gave the man who was glaring at them a withering stare.

"Who is this?" the man asked. He had thinning hair and a pinched expression on his face. He looked at Mary with ill-disguised loathing, and Kane pulled her more fully against his side, under his shoulder. Offering her his protection.

She elbowed him in the ribs, and he frowned at her but did not release her. Mary had always been so ethereal, dancing in and out of his life in a way that made him suspect he'd never be able to hold her for long. He would not waste this opportunity.

"Channing, I'd like you to meet Kane Brentwood. We met when I was living in London. Kane, this is my cousin Channing Moorehead, and his sister Lorette."

He shook hands with both of them. "I'm sorry for your loss."

"We were very close to Uncle David," Lorette said. "We've always lived our lives in an exemplary manner…to show our respect for him."

"We're all impressed, Lorette," Emma said with a touch of sarcasm.

Mary smiled gratefully at her friend, and Kane realized, with his usual sense of great timing where Mary was concerned, he'd bungled into a moment where he shouldn't have. There was a real tension between Mary and her cousins—something not unlike the tension between him and his family.

Lorette turned toward Emma to say something and Mary quietly withdrew, stepping away from the others in the anteroom. The behavior was so unlike the Mary he'd known, but grief did make people vulnerable.

He cupped her elbow and drew her farther away from the others. "What's their problem?"

"Don't worry about it, Kane. It has nothing to do with you."

"I'm not so sure you're right, Mary-Belle. I'm not going to simply walk now that I know we're both free."

"I'm a different woman now, Kane. I have an image to uphold," she said, glancing over her shoulder to make sure that no one was near. "One that makes it impossible to be your mistress."

"What image? I saw your work in a London gallery last spring. Your canvases were always remarkable, but there is something…breathtaking about these new ones."

"Thank you, Kane. But it's not my image as an artist that I'm concerned with. No one here knows anything about that part of my life."

Kane couldn't believe that she'd keep something that was such an integral part of who she was a secret. Mary had lived and breathed painting the entire time they'd been together—almost ten years. He'd had to resort to being her model a time or two to get her attention.

"What image are you concerned with, darling? That of being a mother?"

"No. My child was stillborn," she said softly, and he felt the pain in her words. He wanted to comfort her, but she shook her head.

"I was speaking of the Duvall family image. I came home to claim my heritage, Kane. A heritage that isn't as old as yours but is every bit as stringent. I have to go now. Thanks for coming."

He nodded and let her walk away. He wasn't sure what to make of the new Mary or her words. But one thing was very certain—now that he'd found her, he wasn't leaving Eastwick without laying a claim on her. The kind of claim he should have made when they'd first met, instead of letting his own arrogance force them into roles from which there was no escape.

The funeral wasn't long but went by very slowly for Mary. Afterward, everyone came to the Duvall mansion for the wake. In the midst of the crowd and condolences, Mary retreated to Grandfather David's study for a few moments of solitude. She sat in his big leather chair that smelled faintly of the tobacco he'd always smoked. She inhaled deeply, wrapping her senses in her grandfather's memory.

There was a knock on the door, and Mary knew the interruption signaled she'd been gone from the wake long enough. She answered the summons to find Emma, Caroline and Lily standing there.

"We thought we'd find you hiding out," Emma said, closing the door firmly once they were all inside.

"I'm not hiding," Mary said. Though she suspected her friends knew that she was lying, they'd never call her on it. And she needed time away from the pressure of making nice to all those people. After she was forced to be her society self for too long, she felt an itching deep inside to do something bold and crazy. To shake things up. She had no idea how her friends could survive the daily grind that was society life.

"Not even from Channing? God, that man is an ass," Caroline said.

"Maybe. Is he looking for me? Is that why you came to find me?" Mary asked.

"No Felicity and Vanessa are running interference with Channing, and Abby cornered Lorette. We're here to find out more about that dreamy man with the British accent."

The last thing she wanted to talk about was Kane. She didn't even know where to begin or what to say to her good friends. "That couldn't wait until the next Debs lunch?"

"Who knows when we'll have time for the next one with everyone getting engaged and planning weddings," Caroline said, her eyes glittering with that effervescent joy she brought to everything.

"There's really not much to tell. I met him when I was in London."

"When?" Emma asked.

"My second week there. I was working in Harrods," Mary said. She remembered the way he'd stopped at the display of women's scarves and lingered for almost thirty minutes, never once pretending he was going to buy one but just flirting with her.

"And that's it?" Caroline's voice held a disbelieving tone. "That was ten years ago. The man today looked like he was more to you than a customer."

"He was. We had an…affair," Mary said because she thought her friends would understand that better than knowing that she'd lived in an apartment he'd paid for and that she'd made herself available to him whenever he'd wanted her. She'd been a kept woman.

"I knew there was more between you," Lily said. "There was something about he way he looked at you. And that kiss…"

Mary's lips still tingled, but she was trying very hard to forget that. To forget everything about Kane except the fact that he was no longer a part of her life.

"I haven't seen him in almost three years." To be honest, she didn't want to remember the last time she'd seen Kane.

She'd been so hurt and angry that she'd said something she never should have. When she'd returned to

Eastwick, Grandfather had said that her behavior had caused pain to others and herself, and she'd immediately thought of Kane. If she'd had the comportment then that she had now, maybe things would have turned out differently and she would still have her son…alive today.

"He definitely looked like a man who wanted to rekindle the relationship with you," Caroline stated.

"I can't. Not now. I have too much going on."

"Sure you can," Lily said. "You could at least explore the possibility."

Mary shook her head. Kane wasn't going to be a part of her life again. He was her weakness, and she knew if she allowed him back into her life, she'd have to face her past and the lies she once told. Lies that still haunted her.

Two

Kane was up early the next morning, jogging along the beach of Long Island Sound. He'd spent a restless night trying to come up with something he could use to force Mary back into his life. He knew that it was going to be hard to convince her, but he wasn't a man who was used to failure.

He'd left the family import business when he'd had his marriage to Victoria annulled. His relatives had been appalled that he hadn't done his duty and stayed married to the woman, even though their marriage had been strained from the beginning. At his family's response, Kane had realized that he meant nothing more to them than his role as heir.

He'd taken that opportunity to make a complete break with them.

He'd been living in Manhattan for the last year and a half, where he'd taken a small investment firm and turned it into one of the up-and-comers in the financial world.

He glanced at the horizon, gauging how much farther he'd run before turning back, when he spotted a familiar figure—Mary. She was sitting on the sand and staring out at the ocean. He slowed his pace to a walk to get his breathing under control before he got to her.

"Good morning, darling."

"Morning, Kane," she said, tipping her head back to look up at him. The sun left her face in shadows but brought out the warm highlights in her dark hair. Her locks whipped around her face in the breeze, and in that moment she strongly resembled the woman he'd once known. No longer buttoned-up and perfectly coiffed.

"What are you doing here?"

He put his hands on his hips, standing over her. "Jogging. I'm afraid I'm a bit sweaty. Do you mind if I join you?"

"Would it matter if I said yes?"

"It would." He was a man used to having his way. Things happened for him because he refused to take no for an answer. But with Mary, this time he wanted to be more accommodating. If she didn't want his company, he'd leave.

She rested her chin on her drawn–up knees, staring once again at the ocean and its endlessly cycling waves. "It's a public beach, I can't stop you from sitting."

He dropped to his haunches in front her, his eyes meeting hers. "I'm not interested in the beach, Mary-Belle. I'm interested in your company."

"Why? I thought we hashed this all out years ago," she said, her hands going to her hair and trying to pull it out of her face.

"We didn't," he said, shifting to sink to the sand next to her.

She sighed and the wind carried the sound away from them. He wished that the breeze could as easily clear away their past, yet at the same time he wouldn't give up those years they'd spent together for anything. Just the ending. If he could change the way things had ended he'd be a happier man.

"I can't go back to what we once had," she said.

"I'm not asking you to." He couldn't return either. He was no longer the man he'd been when he'd kept her as his mistress. Now he wanted…hell, he wasn't sure what he wanted aside from Mary back in his bed.

"Oh, well, that's— Why are you here, Kane?"

"Because you are."

"Don't say things like that."

"Even if they are true?"

"Especially if they are true. My life is complicated now. I have family obligations."

"To whom?"

"Grandfather's estate."

He rubbed the back of his neck. It was ironic that now that he was free of family responsibility, she wasn't. "What kind of obligations?"

"It's complicated. I want to use my inheritance to establish a foundation that will help lower-income families. I definitely want to create neonatal units for areas that can't otherwise afford them. And I'd also like to sponsor art programs in schools. I was also thinking to use some property that Grandfather has near the Finger Lakes in New York for a summer camp."

"That sounds ambitious. Where are you going to start?"

"I have no idea. I mean, I'm an artist, not a businessperson. Channing sits on the board of two foundations, so he knows how they operate, but I can't bring myself to ask him to help."

"Why not?"

"Because he and I don't get along. He's hoping I do something outrageous so the money will go to him and Lorette."

"Your inheritance has stipulations?"

"More than you could imagine."

"What kind?"

She made a face at him. "Let's just say that I have to be a model of social behavior."

"Not exactly the Mary I remember."

She tipped her head to the side and gave him a

genuine smile that affected his ability to breathe. He'd never forgotten how beautiful Mary was, but his attraction to her had been more than her physical appearance. It had been the zest she'd had for life. The way her laughter and smiles had filled the empty spaces in *his* life.

"Why are you staring at me, Kane?"

"Because I love your smile."

"My smile?"

He traced his finger down the side of her face, cupping her jaw and rubbing his thumb over her lips. "It's the first thing I noticed about you that day in Harrods."

"My mouth?" she asked, licking her lips, and he almost groaned out loud.

"Yes. Your lips are perfect for kissing."

She flushed a little, nibbling on her lower lip. "Yours are, too."

"Men don't have kissable lips." No one had ever said the things to him that Mary did. She didn't fear his reputation and wasn't intimidated by his wealth and family connections. She'd always treated him as though he were just another guy. And part of him liked the fact that with Mary he could simply be himself.

"Well, you do. Or maybe it's that you really know what you're about when you kiss me."

Her lips parted and her warm breath brushed over his fingers. He leaned down to capture her lips with his. At the contact, she sighed his name, opening her mouth for him. He moved to cradle her head between both of his hands.

He took his time with the kiss, relearning the taste of her and reacquainting her with his taste. He swept his tongue languidly into her mouth, pulling her more firmly into his arms and into his embrace. This was where she belonged.

Kane had always had the ability to transport her from the real world into one where only the two of them existed. In that world she'd do whatever he asked of her and never count the cost. But she couldn't afford to be that cavalier. Not now.

She pulled away from him, easily reading the signs of arousal in the man who'd been her first and only lover.

"Why did you pull away from me?"

"I can't be seen engaging in public displays of affection."

"That suits me. Let's go back to my hotel and engage in private displays of affection."

She shook her head. "Not today. I'm meeting with Grandfather's lawyer at ten. Then I'm interviewing financial planners to find someone to help me establish my trust."

"Who are you meeting with?"

"Someone from Merrill Lynch and someone from A.G. Edwards. I got their names from the phone book," she said. Truth was, she wasn't good with money and she didn't have any idea how to make her dream into reality.

"Would you consider letting me help you?"

Kane was brilliant with investments. He'd carefully invested the money he'd given her during their years together and turned it into a small fortune. She had used that money to support herself before returning to Eastwick. "Do you want to?"

"I wouldn't have offered otherwise," he said with a hint of a grin.

Her question had been inane. "You make it hard for me to think clearly."

"That's good to know."

He stood, offering her his hand and tugging her to her feet. He linked their hands together and started leading her away from the shore, toward her home.

"Will you have breakfast with me?" he asked.

His thumb rubbed over the back of her knuckles, and tingles spread up her arm. Her nipples tightened in response to his touch and his mere proximity. She always reacted this way in his presence. If she had breakfast with him, she'd probably end up making love with him. "No."

"Why not?" he asked, lifting her hand to his mouth and kissing the back of it.

She pulled her hand from his grasp. "I'm not getting involved with you again, Kane. Maybe you shouldn't help me with my inheritance."

"Why not? I'm probably more qualified than some stranger you rang up on the telephone."

"I think working with you will complicate things."

"Things? I'm not sure I understand."

She wanted to punch him in the arm. He frustrated her sometimes and she knew he was doing it deliberately right now. She took a deep breath, remembered that she always had to appear composed.

"I really don't want to give Channing or Lorette a reason to take me to court."

He took her shoulder, pulling her toward his body, wrapping one arm around her waist. He tipped her head back with his other hand, forcing her to look up at him. "I'm not taking no for an answer. I'm back in your life, and we'll take it slowly if that's what you want, but there is no way I'm leaving you again."

"Kane…don't say things like that to me."

"I mean them."

She couldn't reconcile what he was saying to what he'd said when they'd parted. His words still lingered in her mind, the emotional wounds he'd inflicted only half-healed.

"No, you don't. You told me that I was never anything more to you than a mistress, and I believed you. We don't have a great love affair to rekindle. Ours was a business-minded relationship. You paid for my living expenses and I took care of your sexual needs. That was it."

He cursed under his breath but didn't let go of her.

"It was never a business arrangement. Passion like ours can't be contained in something so tame."

Passion…one of her downfalls, if her grandfather was to be believed. Passion had a place only at her easel, where she channeled all of her rebelliousness into her art.

"Passion isn't part of my life now, Kane. You'd do well to remember that. I'm not the woman you knew. I've changed and I can't go back."

"How many times am I going to have to pay for making you my mistress?" he asked, his accent more clipped than normal. He sounded every inch the aristocrat when he talked that way.

"It's not about making you pay. Please, Kane, you have to leave. Go back home and forget about me."

"You may have changed, but I haven't. I'm still a very determined man. And you know I always get what I want."

"Do you have any idea how arrogant you sound?"

"Yes."

That startled a laugh out of her. Kane was still a mix of contradictions. A perfect gentleman in public and a total hedonist in private. She was so tempted to wrap herself around him and let him take her back to those carefree days in London. But she knew that she couldn't.

Something her grandfather had said when she'd returned to Eastwick forbade that. He'd said it was time to grow up and stop running from her responsibilities.

He'd reminded her she was the last Duvall. The only one to carry the mantle of her family's legacy.

"Arrogance isn't going to help you this time," she said, walking away from Kane.

"Yes, it is. You need me to set up this foundation of yours. It's the least I can do for an old friend."

Friend. She didn't know that they'd ever been friends. Friends shared things that she and Kane never had. They'd both played roles and lived in a world of their own making.

"Are you going to deny we were friends?" She heard the challenge in his voice.

"I'm not sure. But I will accept your offer of help. I know you're good with investments and I need someone I can trust."

Mary had a pounding headache after spending three hours in a conference room with her grandfather's attorney, Max Previn, and Channing. Max was a kind, older gentleman who had tried to smooth over the animosity that Channing had brought into the room, but it had been next to impossible.

She'd explained her plans for her inheritance to the lawyer and he'd approved, with the caveat that she remember the stipulations of the will. If at any time she did anything scandalous, the money would be forfeit and she'd have to repay any amount she'd already spent. She'd put the stipulations from her mind long enough to finish the meeting and leave the office.

Mary's car—a late-model Mercedes sedan—was parked at the curb, and she looked at that car feeling a new loathing for this life she'd been forced into. A part of her—the wild, crazy part—wanted to say the hell with it and walk away. She resented the restrictions and the instructions on how to behave that were being dictated from the grave.

But another bigger part of her mourned the baby she'd lost in childbirth, and she wanted to do what she could to ensure that no other woman ever had to live with that crushing feeling.

With her thoughts in such turmoil she couldn't get in the car and go home yet. Instead, she walked along the sidewalk in front of a row of shops until she reached her friend Emma's art gallery. Through the front window Mary could see Emma was with a customer, so she stayed outside. Featured in the display window was her latest print series—Paris. The series was composed of four different pieces that she'd simply titled for each of the seasons.

"Your work has really matured."

She glanced up at Kane, surprised to see him here. He wore a black pullover and a pair of faded jeans. His hair hung rakishly over one eye and he looked way too good. The realization stung because she didn't want to be attracted to him anymore.

"You think so? I still see room for improvement."

"The artist is never satisfied," he said, quoting back her own words.

Why did he remember so much of their time together? She certainly recalled those years in vivid detail, but that wasn't surprising since she'd lived for him for so long. She'd almost refused when he'd offered to set her up as his mistress, uncomfortable with putting herself in that situation. In the end, however, the chance to be with Kane under any circumstances had stayed her.

"What are you doing here?" she asked.

"Waiting for you. I'm going to design a financial plan for your foundation, remember?"

"Of course I remember. I meant, how did you find me here?"

"I was eating lunch across the way and spotted you."

"Oh. For a minute I thought you'd been stalking me."

The droll look on his face made her feel just a little bit foolish. But her response to him underscored something for her. She realized, for her own sanity, she couldn't allow Kane to get close enough to set up her foundation.

"I've changed my mind about accepting your help."

"Why?"

"Channing is going to be watching me like a hawk, trying to find some kind of chink in my new behavior so that he and his family can inherit instead of me."

"Darling, I'm the soul of discretion."

That was true, he always had been. It was her

reaction to Kane that worried her more than anything he would do. That and the secrets of their shared past—both the nature of their relationship and the truth she'd kept from him.

"You don't understand. If they found out I was your mistress, I'd lose everything."

"No one knows the truth except you and I," he said quietly.

She turned away from the window as Emma finished up with her customer. She didn't want her friend to see her with Kane in tow. She took a few steps away from the shop and he followed.

He put his arm around her shoulder, drawing her close to him as he directed them across the street to a small park with a gazebo in the center. Underneath the shade of a large maple tree he stopped, leaning back against the trunk.

"I'm sorry, Mary."

She was taken aback by his words. "For what?"

"For not doing things properly when we first met."

She shook her head. She'd been over their relationship so many times and she knew that a big part of her had liked being Kane's mistress. Had liked that her parents were outraged by it. She closed her eyes at how immature she'd been regardless of how sophisticated she'd felt.

"I think there's plenty of blame to share," she admitted.

He pulled her off balance and into his arms. Mary

was very aware that this was her third public embrace with him and that Channing had actually witnessed the other two.

She pushed against his chest. "Let me go."

"Not this time."

A part of her wanted a relationship with Kane. What had started as a way to outrage her parents and to rebel had turned into love on her part. And she'd never forgotten Kane. But she wasn't ready for the roller coaster of emotions being with him would entail. Especially now with so much at stake.

"I mean it. Let me go. If I'm seen like this, it will give them ammunition to use against me."

"I'll let you go on one condition."

"And that is?"

"You let me work with you to establish the trust."

"It would have to be strictly business. No more touching or kissing. I can't risk it."

"I can't make any promises to not touch you. But I can assure you that I will do my utmost to make sure no one else witnesses it."

"Then my answer will have to be no. Thanks, Kane." She paused. "I know that this sounds weird, but it's been really nice seeing you again."

She turned to walk away, but his low voice stopped her in her tracks. "That's not the answer I was looking for, Mary-Belle."

She glanced over her shoulder at him. He hadn't moved from his relaxed pose against the tree. He looked every bit the brooding English lord she knew him to be.

"Sorry to disappoint you."

"You won't for long. Since you're so concerned about keeping me a secret…I'm going to blackmail you into accepting my help."

Three

Kane watched the blood drain from Mary's face, saw her eyes narrow and her temper flare. He crossed his arms over his chest and waited for her to blast him.

She took two steps toward him and then stopped abruptly, taking several deep breaths, glancing up at the leaves of the maple until she had herself under control. The mask of her composure slipped over her features and the small glimpse he'd had of the real Mary disappeared.

"Who would you tell?"

"I think I'd start with your cousins."

"I don't believe you," she stated boldly.

Kane didn't believe it himself, but he knew he

couldn't let her walk away so easily again. Desperate times called for desperate measures, and all that. "It wouldn't be a decision I made lightly. But I'm not going to allow you to dismiss me from your life."

"Kane, please."

He'd heard those words from her so many different times. In the bedroom when she was begging him to touch her breasts. In that run-down flat in Paris that she'd fled to when he'd gotten engaged. And now when he was blackmailing her. He fought to keep focused on the end result: helping Mary and winning back a place in her life.

"I'm a different person now."

"I can see that," he said, catching a strand of her dark hair between his fingers. Her hair was still softer than silk, but now it was cut to her shoulders and straight, with none of the wild curls she used to have. It was one more thing about Mary that was so foreign to him, that he had to figure out what had caused the change.

"I want to get to know the new Mary. I'm a different man, too."

"You still seem arrogant to me."

"I am."

He wanted her. He'd been in a constant state of semiarousal since he'd read her name in the newspaper. Seeing her had brought all the lust to life in him.

"So what's it to be?" he asked.

She wrapped her arms around her waist and

glanced down at the ground. After a few moments she looked up at him. "I guess you can help me."

He felt a surge of triumph and absolutely no guilt. He wasn't about to let anything harm Mary again. As it was, she looked a little pale and her face was drawn. He knew that the process of grieving was a hard one, and Mary didn't seem to be taking care of herself. She was thinner than he'd ever seen her.

"Have you had lunch?"

"Um…what?" she asked, narrowing her eyes at him.

"Have you eaten?" He carefully enunciated each word.

He was rewarded for his silliness with a tiny smile.

"No, I haven't."

"Then we'll discuss the details of how to get started on your trust over lunch."

"Didn't you already eat?"

"Yes."

"I'll be fine. We can go back to Grandfather's—I mean, my house—and I'll grab a salad there."

"You're the boss."

"I wish. You aren't the type to let a woman tell you what to do," she said, walking across the park toward the parking lot.

"You're right," he said, falling into step beside her. "But I do always consider your desires."

She flushed. He knew her well enough to know the look on her face meant she was thinking of sex. His personality was dominant in the bedroom and out. He remembered building her to the edge of climax time and again, then waiting for her sweet cries of frustration before he finally plunged deep into her body and brought them both the relief they desperately needed.

He wrapped his arm around her waist, causing her to stop. She tipped her head back to look at him, and he noted that her pupils were dilated and her breathing was a little heavier than it had been earlier. "Do you want me, Mary-Belle?"

She opened her mouth, her small pink tongue darting out to wet her lips. "Yes."

That one little word washed over him like a satin glove on his naked skin. His blood pumped harder, his erection stirred, and his entire body longed for her. It had been too long since he'd last sated himself in her curvy body, and he wanted—no, needed—to do so again.

He lowered his head to taste her, to make up for the hurt he'd caused earlier when he'd threatened her. He'd never have the words she wanted to hear, but he would always show her with his actions what he really felt.

Their lips barely brushed. He rubbed his over hers, building the moment between them, knowing that they couldn't go much further than this one little kiss. But later, after she'd eaten and they'd discussed business…then he'd deliver on the promise of this one small kiss. Vaguely he registered the sound of footsteps behind them.

"Third time, Mary."

Kane pulled back from her ready to deck her cousin. She turned in Kane's arms—not pulling away from him—to face her cousin.

"I thought you had a company to run, Channing. I know that your inheritance is tied to the profit of Duvall-Moorehead Manufacturing. Aren't you afraid that skulking around after me is going to distract you?"

"I can handle my job *and* keep an eye on you."

"That's not your job, Moorehead," Kane said.

"Is it yours?"

"That's irrelevant. Anyone who threatens Mary will have to go through me first."

Mary led the way into the kitchen, very aware of Kane's heavy footsteps behind her. She felt so out of control, and for the first time since she'd come back to Eastwick she was glad of Grandfather's lessons in composure. The old Mary would have skipped lunch, grabbed Kane's hand and led him to her bedroom.

But now she thought about the consequences of her rash actions, what would be lost and what would be gained. So instead she was heading toward her sunny kitchen, intent on the mundane task of eating a salad.

She'd simmered all the way home thinking of the way that Channing and Kane had reacted to each other. She really was sick of the men in her life thinking she needed them to fight her battles.

Carmen, the Duvall family housekeeper, was in

the kitchen when Mary entered. "Good afternoon, Carmen."

"Good afternoon, Miss Mary. Can I help you with something?"

"I'd like a salad and some tea brought into the study. Kane, do you want anything?"

"Perrier, please."

"I'll bring it in."

Mary waited until they were in the study with the door closed before she addressed Kane again.

"I don't want you fighting my battles."

"Too bad."

"Kane, I'm serious about this. Channing is going to be around the rest of my life and, when you're gone, that kind of macho display is going to come back to haunt me."

"What makes you think I'll be gone?"

She didn't let herself dwell on those words. She ignored him, turning away and seating herself behind the desk. Her life was in flux right now. She'd experienced this type of soul-changing, life-altering event twice before. Each time it had involved a complete upheaval of everything she knew about herself and the world around her.

And each time Kane had somehow come into her life. But he never stayed. No matter how content or happy they were together, he always had one foot out the door. She'd come to accept that she was meant to spend her life alone. Not like the women in the

Debs Club, who were pairing up like animals on Noah's ark. Mary had always been a little different, and her life's path was, too.

"Ignoring me won't make me go away."

"I'm not ignoring you," she said, tossing her head and gathering her thoughts. She could never completely ignore Kane. His blatant masculinity dominated whatever space he occupied. He tempted her to forget about trusts and cousins and family and…to act like a fool again?

"You're here to work, right?" she asked, angry at herself for being so weak where he was concerned. Sometimes it really ticked her off that the only man she'd allowed herself to fall in love with was someone who could never live with her in a normal way. She wondered what that said about her.

"That's one reason."

"The only one that counts."

"If you say so."

"I do."

He took a seat across from her, pulling out a notepad from the briefcase he carried. She hadn't noticed the case earlier but did so now. She'd helped him pick it out.

"I made a few phone calls earlier and have set up a meeting for us with an attorney friend of mine. He'll talk us through the legalities of what you want to do."

Kane was a thorough man, so she wasn't surprised that he'd already started working on setting up her trust. And she knew this wasn't just business to him. For a minute she wanted to bask in the feeling of being cherished and taken care of. That was one of the reasons she'd stayed with him so long. He'd been the first person in her life to actually take care of her.

True, she'd taken care of all his sexual needs in exchange, rendering their relationship in terms of an agreement. Had she reneged on her agreement with her parents? Had they never approved of her because she'd never even tried to be the daughter they'd wanted her to be? That was a path to pursue another time.

"Thanks. We need to have a contingency built into the investment plan in case I have to pay back my inheritance."

"Why would you have to do that?"

"The will has some stipulations, remember?"

"When will the money be available to you?"

"Mr. Previn has okayed a release of the funds in three months' time. But I'll have a probationary period that will last for the following two years."

"Probationary period? What exactly are they watching you for?"

"Behavior. I'm supposed to follow the rules of comportment that were written by my great-grandmother. The rules were revised by both my grandmother and my own mother."

Kane didn't say anything and she was glad for it. She hated that stupid comportment book. She hated how every detail of her childhood had been used as an example of what not to do in her mother's version of the book.

"Sounds like a long line of rules."

He had no idea. They were stringent, too. No room for mistakes in the Duvall family. Her mother had once told Mary that she'd felt the mantle of expectation on her own shoulders once she'd married Mary's father. But to Mary that mantle had always felt like a choke hold.

"You know how family is. Your own has rules, as well."

"They don't apply to me anymore."

"Why not?" she asked. The past three years she'd deliberately cut herself off from anything that would carry information about Kane. She hadn't read the *Globe* or talked to any of the friends she had in London. It had been too painful to think of him in a new relationship with another woman, the two of them living a life together.

"When I divorced Victoria I was told to never come back again."

"Why did you divorce her?"

"That has nothing to do with your investments."

"You're right. I'm sorry, Kane. I had no right to pry."

He set down his notepad and came to where she sat, leaning one hip against the huge walnut desk. "I wouldn't deny you anything you ask for. But you were very adamant about keeping this afternoon all about business."

"I guess I was."

"Changed your mind?" he asked, stroking one finger down her face.

"I'm not sure."

Kane lifted Mary from the chair and set her on the edge of the desk. He pushed her thighs apart and stepped between her legs. Sliding his hands down her back, he grabbed her butt and pulled her forward until he could nestle his erection against the center of her body.

She gripped his upper arms and tipped her head back.

"What do you think you're doing?" she asked, leaning toward him.

"Convincing you to change your mind," he said, letting his gaze drift down her body, lingering on her breasts and her taut nipples pushing against her blouse. He remembered the way she looked—the curves of her breasts, the dark pink color of her nipples. He remembered how sensitive she was to all kinds of stimulation.

"Looks like my plan is working," he said, his eyes reconnecting with hers.

"You have a plan for sex."

"Darling, this is so much more than sex."

She closed her eyes. "I hope so."

He didn't know what to say to that. So he lowered his head and took her mouth with his. He slipped one hand into her silky hair, holding her head at the angle that gave him full access to her mouth.

He ran his tongue over her lips, teasing the both of them. Her breath brushed over his tongue as she opened her mouth, inviting him inside. But he waited. Anticipation turned her on, and this was all about Mary.

She shifted against him, a subtle movement of her hips that brought her against the tip of his shaft. He moaned and bit her lower lip in retaliation. He sucked on it to soothe the sting from his teeth and she undulated against him.

The tips of her breasts brushed against his chest, and he wished they were both naked so he could feel her nipples against his flesh.

He slipped his tongue into her mouth for a quick foray, pulling back when she tangled her tongue with his. She shifted her head, trying to move closer to him, but he held her still.

For this one moment he was in control of her. Or so he thought, until he felt her fingers at his neck, her nails scraping down under his shirt collar.

He stopped teasing them both and took her mouth in the kiss he'd been wanting since he'd first seen her again. He thrust his tongue deep inside and let his instincts take over. He stopped thinking and analyzing. Stopped worrying about wooing her and keeping his cool.

No man could be cool around Mary. She was fire and passion. The kind of heat he'd never felt before…

and never would again. She warmed that cold part of him that no one else even realized he had.

His tongue and mouth took hers the way he needed to take her body again. He wanted to reestablish the physical bond between them. To bind her to him as tightly as he could so that she'd never leave him again.

He slowly unbuttoned her blouse. When he had them undone, he pushed the cloth away from her body and put his palm over her breast, loving the full weight of it.

He slipped his hand under the lacy demi-cup of her bra and then paused, savoring the sensation of skin on skin. She twisted her mouth from under his, her breathing hard, her breasts straining.

He leaned back to stare down at her body almost revealed to him. The earth shifted around him and he wondered how he'd ever be content with just a kiss.

Sliding his hands over the smooth skin of her stomach and midriff, he kept his eyes on her. She watched him, watched his big hands move over her small body.

He took her mouth with his once more, even as he knew he couldn't take this any further. Her house-keeper would be coming down the hall any moment, and he didn't want Mary to be embarrassed by anything that passed between the two of them.

Before he could stop himself, he leaned down to kiss the white swell of her breast near the edge of her bra. His tongue swept under the cloth and brushed her nipple quickly. But she tasted so good he couldn't resist tugging the fabric aside with his teeth and sucking her deep into his mouth.

Her hands framed his head, and his world narrowed to this woman and her arousal. He wanted her aroused to the point where she couldn't think of anything but the two of them together.

She moaned and shifted against him, wrapping one thigh around his hips. He lifted his head, glancing down at her. Her exposed nipples were wet and hard from his kisses, the flush of desire making her skin rosy.

He'd never seen Mary more beautiful than she was right now. He twisted his hips between her legs, bringing the tip of his erection in direct contact with her. He used his hands on her butt to rock her, creating a tantalizing friction between them. Her eyes closed and she rubbed herself voluptuously against him.

He kept up the rhythm, kissing her until he felt her jerk against him. She cried out his name as her orgasm rolled through her body. He embraced her against his chest and buried his face in the curve of her neck. He took deep breaths and tried desperately to hold back his own climax.

As the physical sensations ran riot through him, he came to one conclusion. There was no way he was walking away from this woman again. No matter what happened.

Four

Mary jerked out of Kane's arms and headed for the door. What the hell was she thinking? She couldn't give in to the passion between them. She'd known deep inside that Kane was dangerous to her, that the way he made her feel and act would be her downfall…again.

Her body was still on fire for him, and she wanted nothing more than to make love with him. Here, in this room, where she'd endured the most blistering reprimands throughout her life.

The cool air on her breasts made her realize she was still exposed. She pulled the cups of her bra over her aroused flesh and buttoned her blouse.

"Mary." He said her name quietly but with the kind of authority that made her stop.

But she didn't turn around. She couldn't. She needed to leave the room and his presence right now before she gave in to her wild side and did something she would later regret. Letting Kane back into her bed would be one such regret. The secrets she still kept and the truth she wasn't ready to revisit guaranteed it.

"I—I think we've covered enough for today. Any further discussions can be made over the phone or in the presence of other people. Please see yourself out."

She left the room at a clipped pace, heading down the hallway and outside to the beautifully landscaped gardens that once had been her grandfather's refuge and now had become her own. She didn't stop at the pool or the guesthouse cabana but kept walking until she found the old weeping willow tree that had stood on the grounds for years.

The long branches hung to the ground, providing a private sanctuary within. Mary pushed them aside and sat on the small marble bench nestled against the trunk. This was the place she'd always escaped to—a protected spot where no one from the mansion could see her and she could let go.

Tears burned the back of her eyes and she wanted to rail out loud against life. When was it going to get easier? She knew she was on the verge of whining, but she had worked so hard to change her life, to put the sins of her past behind her so that she could make a new start, one that would live up to the Duvall family name. And she'd thought she'd succeeded.

But now she knew the truth.

She hadn't changed at all. She hadn't made the great strides she'd believed she had. No, she was still the same wild child inside.

"Mary."

She glanced up at the sound of Kane's voice to see him standing just inside the willow branches. In her private sanctuary. Where no one else dared to follow her.

She felt a dampness on her cheeks and realized only then that the tears she'd been holding back had fallen. She wiped the wetness away.

"I believe I asked you to leave."

He sat on the bench next to her, casually resting the ankle of his right foot on his left knee. He seemed like a man with no worries and all the time in the world.

"Please, Kane. Just leave."

"Do you really want that?" he asked. "I'm not convinced that you will be happier without me."

She had no idea. She only knew that Kane complicated a situation that was already tricky. "Honestly I'm not sure. But it's not your job to make me happy."

"Of course it is. I'm responsible for hurting you. I have to make up for that."

"When did you hurt me?"

"In Paris."

She closed her eyes, remembering that time. It had

been April and she'd been so ecstatic to see Kane. Ever since she'd learned she was pregnant with their child, she'd been hoping he'd come to find her. To tell her he wasn't marrying his proper English lady. Instead…well, suffice it to say that she'd believed in happily ever after until Paris.

"I don't want to talk about that time."

"I want to make up for what I did."

"You can't. We have to leave those experiences in the past and move on."

"I don't know if I can. I was so jealous when I realized you had a new man in your life and you were pregnant with his child. I know I said some cruel things."

There had been no other lover. She'd never found another man she wanted to touch her the way Kane had. She'd made up that lie when she'd realized that he wasn't leaving Victoria and that the only reason he'd sought her was to ask her to continue being his mistress. She'd been hurt and angry and had lashed out.

"I think we both have regrets of that time."

He smiled then, just briefly, and put his arm around her shoulder, drawing her to his side. He relaxed when she nestled close. Mary hadn't realized how tense Kane was.

When she looked up at him she was surprised to find him staring at her. "Why are you here, Kane? Really?"

He didn't reply for so long that she thought maybe he wouldn't. She wasn't sure why his motives were important, but they were. It seemed to her as though Kane was pursuing her again. Whether she wanted to admit it or not, Kane was the one man that haunted her dreams. The one man who made her forget who she was. The one man who could make her surrender on every level.

"I'm here for you, Mary-Belle. I want you in my life."

"As your mistress?" she asked, overlooking his assertion of support.

He cursed under his breath. "No, not as my mistress."

They were words she would have given anything to hear three years ago, but now she wasn't sure what they meant. And she was too fragile emotionally to ask him right now. But she would later.

"Why now?" she asked.

"I've been searching for you since the day my marriage to Victoria was annulled."

She wasn't sure she believed him. Kane wasn't a man to pine over a woman. "Why was it annulled? I thought you were divorced."

"It's a bit complicated."

Kane held Mary in his arms, fearing for the first time that he might fail in winning her back. There were parts of his life he'd always hidden from the world and his family. And then there were the parts he'd hidden from Mary. Despite his reticence, she was still the person he'd been the most honest with. But now…he didn't know if he could open up the way she wanted him to.

His marriage to Victoria had been wrong from the beginning. But he'd wanted to please his parents, to live up to their expectations just once.

"Tell me about the complicated part of your marriage." Mary's words pulled him from his thoughts.

"Have I ever mentioned my older brother?" he asked even though he knew he hadn't told her. His feelings for Nigel were also complicated. Nigel had been killed in an avalanche while climbing Mount Everest when Kane was twenty-one.

"No. We didn't talk much about family during our time together, did we?"

He suspected that she had liked the idea that they were just two lovers without ties, without commitments, as much as he had. Mary had been bent on escape the same way he had been. She'd left her old life behind when she'd left her country. And he'd run away from his life with her.

"You were an oasis for me, Mary-Belle," he said, rubbing his jaw against the softness of her hair.

"An oasis? That's almost poetic," she said.

It came to him that he needed her to understand she was more important to him than his family or his business interests. It had taken losing her for him to realize how much of himself was tied up in her, how much of himself she'd taken with her.

"Tell me about Nigel," she said. "Are you and he similar?"

"No, he was everything I wasn't. The perfect son, really, and a natural leader—everything my parents could have wished for in a son. He was groomed from childhood to take my father's place as the head of the family business."

"Why were you running it when we met?" she asked.

"Nigel was killed during a climbing expedition. We were all devastated."

She wrapped her arms around him and held him. "You did what you could to step into his role?"

"Yes."

Mary contemplated him with those vivid blue eyes of hers. "I'm not sure what this has to do with your marriage."

Kane took a deep breath, forcing himself to concentrate on the story he was telling instead of on Mary herself. But it was damned hard. "Victoria was engaged to Nigel. When my brother was alive, she was a different person." He didn't like to think about the changes Nigel's death had wrought in her. "Afterward, she was in a deep depression for a long time."

"So you stepped in and offered to marry her?"

"Not at first. I just visited her regularly and we would talk about Nigel. Eventually she started getting out of bed and leaving her room. I took her out a few times, and the next thing I knew, we were engaged."

"Did you take her out while we were together?" she asked.

If he articulated what he'd felt in those days, how pompous and arrogant he'd been, thinking about having both the proper British wife and the wild, sexy mistress, Mary would leave him. But he was done with lying. When his marriage had ended, he'd left behind everything familiar to him—all of his parents' old expectations—and started over as his own man.

And that man was determined to win Mary back, to offer her a place in his life that wasn't hidden in shadows or secrets.

"Yes," he said.

She pulled away from him and he saw the fire in her eyes. He braced himself for her anger. "You arrogant SOB."

She stomped away from him, her entire being radiating her anger. She clenched and unclenched her fists at her sides. He watched her struggle to control her temper.

"Don't stop. I was arrogant and a total ass. I'm so sorry."

She faced him again, her arms crossed under her breasts. "Yes, you were a huge jackass."

She took several deep breaths, and he saw her lips move as she counted to ten. Not once but three times before she finally said, "Finish telling me about your marriage. Why did you get an annulment?"

Kane faced her and tried to find a way to explain

his marriage to someone who hadn't been inside their very cold, very polite house. It was next to impossible, but maybe Mary would understand.

And she deserved to know what he'd left her for. "Before the avalanche, Nigel called me from the base camp and made me promise to take care of his fiancée if anything happened to him. At the time I didn't think anything of it, but afterward…" His words trailed off as he remembered. With effort he pulled himself back. "The truth is, Victoria and I never consummated our marriage."

"You were married for at least a year," Mary stated. "I can't imagine you going without sex for that long."

"How do you know that?"

"I kept track of you after we parted…until I started to despise myself for that weakness."

He hated himself in that moment for what he'd put them both through. "I'm sure your husband must have enjoyed that."

"It was my guilty secret, Kane. Like everything about you, it was hidden from the real world."

"That's why I'm back. I want a chance at a real relationship—an open relationship with you, Mary. A chance to make up for the pain I caused before. And I hope that you'll be able to forgive me in time."

"I can't do this now. Maybe in a few years, when I've established myself here in Eastwick, but not now."

"I can't wait a few years. Our lives are slipping

away and you are the one person I want to share mine with."

He closed the distance between them to take her in his arms. She resisted for a moment before leaning into his chest. He held her tightly to him. "I'm going to do everything in my power to prove to you I'm a new man. An honest man. One worthy not only of your body but also of your love."

For the rest of the afternoon Mary felt like a huge fraud. She had a secret that would hurt Kane as much as the knowledge that he'd dated another woman while she'd been his mistress had affected her. But Mary kept her mouth shut for now.

After their passionate encounter in the study and then the emotional discussion they'd had under the willow tree, she wanted to find some semblance of normalcy.

Carmen set up their drinks and Mary's lunch on a table near the pool. Mary realized that the housekeeper must have figured out she and Kane were fighting. Darn it, she wasn't doing a good job of appearing serene. That was what the therapist that Grandfather had sent her to had told her to strive for—the appearance of serenity.

When she'd told her grandfather why the Duvall inheritance was so important, explaining to him about the baby she'd lost, he'd understood and approved of her plans. But he'd cautioned her that she had to show some signs of carrying on the traditions started by the Duvall women three generations earlier. And that meant being a role model to young women. Since then she'd been slowly figuring out how to comport herself according to those strict rules. And it had never been so difficult as it had since Kane's return.

Mary sighed and took the last bite of her salad. Kane stood as soon as she was finished. "Want to go for a walk on the beach?"

"I'm not exactly dressed for a walk on the beach."

"I'll wait while you change."

"The cabanas are stocked with swimsuits and beachwear if you'd like to change, as well."

"I will. I'll meet you back here in fifteen minutes."

She changed into a long summer skirt and a wraparound sleeveless top. She started barefoot for the stairs, luxuriating in the cold feel of the tile and then the thick pile of the Berber carpet on the landing beneath her feet. She stopped for a minute, rubbing her toes on the carpet, before she remembered that she was supposed to always wear shoes. The weight of *supposed to, have to* and *should* settled on her, threatening to overwhelm her with guilt and responsibility.

She ran back to her room and found a pair of walking sandals before racing down the stairs as quickly as she could. Sometimes running was the only way she could get rid of the emotions inside her.

She skidded to stop on the bottom step when she

heard Carmen speaking to Channing. Mary hesitated, not wanting to have to speak to her cousin again. She slipped her shoes off and then quickly dashed around the corner and out onto the patio, running full-out.

She ran into Kane, who prevented her fall with his hands on her waist.

"What are you running from?" he asked, his hold on her sliding from her waist to her hips. There was a scant inch of space between their bodies.

"My cousin. I don't want to have to deal with him again today."

Kane dropped his hands and stepped away from her. "I'll take care of him."

She stopped him with a hand on his arm. Though Kane was a very sophisticated man who gave the appearance of being a suave gentleman, she knew him to be a first-rate amateur boxer. And Channing wasn't. As much as she wanted her cousin off her back, she didn't want to see him beaten to accomplish that.

"No, Kane. Let's just go on our walk."

"Are you sure?"

"Yes. Remember what I said about you not fighting my battles?"

"I remember everything you say," he said, taking her shoes from her hands and going down on one knee to help her into them.

He stood, took her hand in his big, warm one, then tugged her toward the path that led down to the beach. She walked beside him somewhat bemused by his attitude.

"What was that about?"

He pulled his sunglasses from his pocket and put them on. Scanning the path ahead of them, he didn't look at her. "I want to take care of you."

There was something in his voice that told her she was missing an important element to what he was saying. And it had more to do with something Kane felt than whatever he was revealing.

"I don't need you to do that," she said. She'd been on her own most of her life. Even when she'd been Kane's mistress she'd lived a solitary existence.

"Part of my mind acknowledges that, but there's this other part that won't listen. You seem so fragile now."

"Fragile? Kane Brentwood, I'm never fragile," she said. She'd always been a solid person both in terms of her physical being and in terms of her personality. She hated that any part of her vulnerability might be obvious to Kane or, worse, the world. "You're probably just seeing my new, more mature behavior."

"I don't think so."

"Why not?"

"I never thought of you as immature before. There's this difference in your eyes now, Mary. A sadness that I want to help lighten."

Her breath caught deep in her body and she had to look away from his penetrating gaze. That sorrow he saw was the grief that lingered from the loss of her child. The grief that not even two and a half years of distance could dull. The grief that she suspected Kane would feel, as well, if he learned the truth of her baby's parentage.

"I don't think anything you do will be able to change that," she said.

"That's not going to stop me trying. I'm going to do everything right this time—romance and wooing, not just sex."

"You're off to a rocky start if that interlude in the study was any indication."

"That's hardly my fault."

"How do you figure?"

"You're a siren, Mary-Belle. A temptress. And I'm defenseless against your pull."

She wanted to warn him that she wasn't the woman he thought she was, but walking hand in hand with him on the beach was too close to the secret dreams she'd once harbored to disturb it. She kept quiet and nurtured a ray of hope deep inside that this time she and Kane would last.

Five

Spending so much time with Mary over the past week was torture on Kane's libido, but it was worthwhile. He savored the emotions she evoked in him, feeling truly alive for the first time in more than three years.

Tonight he'd invited her to dinner at the house he was renting. He'd employed a small house staff and had just finished pouring himself a martini when his butler led Mary into the living room.

She wore a slim-fitting sheath dress that left her arms bare. Around her neck she wore a strand of pearls that he'd given her. Her hair hung in soft waves to her shoulders and she'd tucked the left side behind her ear.

She wore minimal makeup—just something shiny

on her lips that drew his eyes to them. For a moment he couldn't look away, then realized he was staring.

"You look lovely."

"Thank you. I'm sorry I'm a few minutes late. Max called to tell me about a meeting that Channing and Lorette have asked for tomorrow morning at ten and Max was briefing me on what to expect."

"Do you want me to attend?" He had two meetings in the morning—a conference call at nine-thirty that he could probably reschedule and a lunch that he didn't want to move. It was with a real estate agent to visit some business properties; he was planning to move his offices to Eastwick now that Mary would be part of his life again.

"No, I want to do it myself. I have the presentation about the trust that you put together, so I'll take that."

"If you change your mind, I'm close by." He'd once kept their lives carefully separate and he was determined to be accessible this time. It was important to him that Mary see the differences.

"Why did you rent this place?" she asked, making a slow journey around the room before stopping in front of the stone fireplace that dominated one entire wall. She touched the cold stones and he had a glimpse of the sensuous Mary who spent all of her time indulging her senses.

"Commuting was taking too much time. And we could never have drinks and dinner like this."

"Like what?" she asked, tilting her head and

giving him a flirty smile that caused an immediate reaction in him.

God, he wanted this woman. He could scarcely think when they were in the same room. His erection was full, pulsing, pressing against the zipper of his pants. He constantly watched her, waiting for an opening to touch her, any innocent excuse he could find.

"*Alone.* Your house is full of people all the time." Her friends and their new husbands or fiancés were always stopping by. They hadn't been overly welcoming to him until Mary had made it clear she wanted him in her house. Since then he'd been slowly easing his way into the circle of her friends. He'd quickly learned how seriously she took the bond of friendship. Her friends from the Debs Club—a name Mary had explained had come from their younger years as debutantes—were immediately granted Mary's full attention whenever they asked.

"Sorry about that. My friends are an important part of my life."

"I wasn't complaining. I simply wanted a night of you to myself."

"I thought you said this time we weren't all about sex."

"Did I really? I must have been temporarily insane when I said that."

"Is that why we're having martinis? Hoping to get me drunk enough to say yes?"

"Never. Though if it were to happen, I'd try to be noble."

"I have a feeling *noble* wouldn't last very long," she said with a laugh.

It was the first time he'd seen her so open and he was completely charmed.

"I want a chance for us to be reacquainted with each other."

"I approve."

He arched one eyebrow at her. "I'm glad to hear my plan is working. We have about thirty minutes until dinner will be served. Would you like to go out on the deck?"

Kane's house was a split-level with the main entry and living spaces on the second floor.

"I'd love to."

He bent and took the kiss he'd been dying for since she'd entered the room. She set her drink on the nearby table and turned more fully into his embrace. Her hands held his head still while she tipped her own head to the side, angling for deeper penetration. One of his hands rested on her shoulder, his thumb tracing the line of skin exposed by the scoop neckline of her dress.

He struggled to let her control the moment. If he had his way, dinner would be late—much later—and they'd spend the rest of the evening on the soft rug in front of the fireplace.

Finally he gave up his struggle. He set down his

glass, snaked his arm around her waist and lifted her off balance, effectively shifting the power in the embrace to him. He plundered her mouth, taking it the way he longed to take her body.

His free hand slid between their bodies, caressing her breasts through the silk of her dress. He moaned as he encountered only her dress.

"Are you wearing a bra?"

"Can't you tell?"

"Are you trying to make me crazy?"

"Yes," she said, wriggling against him. "I'm wearing a garter belt and stockings, too."

He set her on her feet and took a step away from her. "Do you want to have dinner tonight?"

"Yes."

"Then you need to go outside for a few minutes."

"By myself?"

"Yes."

He pushed her toward the balcony and strode out of the room. Teasing each of them with anticipation was one thing, outright seduction something else. It seemed Mary had her own agenda and Kane needed to make sure everything was perfect if they were to end up in his bed tonight.

Mary sipped her martini, trying to still her nerves. Things weren't as rosy as she'd painted to Kane. Somehow her cousins had found out that she hadn't been married when she'd given birth to her son,

Brent. And now they were determined to find out who the father was.

She took another sip of her drink. The sinking feeling in her stomach made her feel as though she was losing control of the carefully constructed new Mary. She knew it was only a matter of time before they tracked down Jean-Paul Bertrand the gallery owner with whom she'd lived with when she'd fled to Paris.

Jean-Paul would cover for her, she knew that. He'd been too good a friend not to. But she also knew that Albert, Jean-Paul's live-in lover, couldn't tolerate lying and wouldn't lie for her. She felt terrible because she hated his damned honesty.

She finished the martini in one long swallow, glancing out at the water and wishing that, just once, her life would be uncomplicated.

If it were only the inheritance that would be affected, she'd walk away. Kane had been showing her a financial investment plan that would enable her to fund the trust without her grandfather's money. But she knew that Channing and Lorette weren't going to be satisfied with only her leaving—they wanted her to never come back.

When they discovered the truth about Brent's paternity, they'd leak it to a newspaper or some other very public source. She bit her bottom lip and closed her eyes. Not only would the scandal be disastrous for her but also Kane would find out everything—and not from her, as he should.

She had to tell him. All of it. And then…then he'd realize that he wasn't the only one who had something to make up for.

The man had gone to extraordinary lengths to seduce his way back into her life. And not only with sex, which had been the driving factor in their life before, but with a commitment of every little detail of his life.

He'd rented this house to be close to her and, as a result, had done some horrific commuting to his office over the past week. Instead of passing her trust account to a junior partner, Kane had carved the time out of his schedule to handle it personally.

He'd even set about charming her friends and making a place for himself in the circle of her life.

"Ready for a refill?" he asked, coming up behind her and placing his hand on the small of her back. She felt his touch as though the silk of her clothes weren't there.

"Yes," she said. Another Grey Goose martini was exactly what the doctor ordered.

Or maybe not. Getting drunk might not be the best method of gathering her courage to tell Kane the truth.

"Have I thanked you for all your help with setting up my trust?"

"Yes, many times. Aren't you glad I insisted on helping?"

"I'm not sure I should say yes." So much of her current anxiety stemmed directly from the fact that he was in her life and that he would be affected by whatever her cousins uncovered about her past.

He leaned over her, his big body filling her sight, and tenderly brushed his lips against her forehead. "It's okay, darling, we both know that you are."

She wrapped her arm around his waist and laid her head on his chest. The steady beating of his heart under her ear was reassuring. He enfolded her within his arms, and she felt completely surrounded by him. Completely protected by him. She knew it was an illusion, but she wished it were real. She wished that he was her reward for behaving the way her grandmother and mother had always wanted her to.

He tipped her head back with one finger under her chin and kissed her as if he had all the time in the world. When he lifted his mouth, she stared up at him, bemused by this man.

"Do you always have to be right?" she asked, keeping her tone light, but she feared she'd made things worse by accepting his help. She'd never really gotten over Kane. She'd shut down her emotions after losing her son, forced them deep inside her so she'd stop aching. Seeing Kane again made her remember that she'd closed herself off from many good emotions as well as the sad ones.

He shrugged his broad shoulders. "I'm glad you think I'm always right."

"Name one time when you weren't?" she asked, not believing Kane had ever not made the right decision. Or if he'd made a mistake, that he'd eventually come out the winner.

He rubbed her back and then stepped away from her. "When I let you go."

"I'll agree with that, but let's not make this about us tonight. I want to know more about the real Kane Brentwood."

"Ah, you're after my secrets." He took her empty glass into the living room.

She followed him, leaning against the open doorway and watching the way he moved. He'd always fascinated her. She itched for a pad and charcoal pencil to sketch him. It had been so long since she'd felt the urge to do anything artistic.

"Do you have so many?" she asked.

"Don't we all?"

"I asked about you."

"So you did. Well, I'm not sure I'm ready to be that honest with you. I prefer to have you thinking of me as a slayer of dragons."

"Going to slay my dragons?"

"At the very least, I'll slay your cousins."

She smiled at him. He refilled their martini glasses and then rejoined her outside. The setting sun cast long shadows on the balcony, and the breeze from the ocean was warm. Mary turned her face to it and let her cares be swept away. She knew she was postponing her problems, that they'd still be waiting for her in the morning. But she wanted this one night with Kane. One night with the man she was falling for again.

* * *

Mary was a little tipsy from the martinis. Kane was enchanted by seeing a blend of the old Mary he remembered and the new conservative model of perfection. She flirted with him, arousing and exciting him.

At the moment, they were discussing movies, having already covered books. Since they knew each other's likes, there was none of that exploring of tastes that new couples did. Instead they debated each other's favorites and recent discoveries. He'd been surprised that she'd read the latest military history book written by a British scholar. It wasn't her usual type of book, and he wondered if it meant that she'd missed him before his reappearance in her life.

"What do you think of those actresses with pouty lips?" she asked.

He rubbed his jaw, pretending to think about something he'd never noticed before. To him, all women paled in comparison to Mary. He was damned lucky if he could remember any other woman when she was around.

"I've never really considered it."

"Are you sure? What if I had those injections?" She did an exaggerated pout to demonstrate.

As always when he looked at her mouth, he wanted to kiss it. "I think you have the most kissable mouth on the planet."

"Really? Did you know that on Valentine's Day

there was a kissing contest that broke the Guinness world record for most couples kissing at the same time?"

"No, I didn't know that."

"I read about it. Grandfather said all that public affection wasn't a good idea. That passions might be stirred—" She flushed as if recognizing where she was leading this conversation and looked away.

"Your grandfather had a good point."

Kane was beginning to realize that there was more than seduction on Mary's mind tonight. In all the years he'd known her, he'd seen her smashed only twice. Once, on the day she'd heard the news of her parents' and brother's deaths, and the second on the day he'd told her he was getting married to another woman.

Damn. If he'd been thinking with his head instead of his libido, he would have seen something was wrong with her. Reading Mary's moods wasn't as easy as it once had been. Where she used to be as mercurial as the North Sea, now she had the surface tranquility of the Caribbean.

"Where is all this talk of kissing leading?"

"To bed," she said, licking her lips and leaning forward. "That is what you've been wanting, isn't it?"

"Only when you want it, too."

She sighed, pushed her chair away from the table and walked over to him with a gait that was anything but steady.

He shoved his chair back, getting to his feet as she approached, but she pushed him into the chair and sat on his lap.

"I do want you, Kane. I never stopped wanting you. No matter how angry or hurt I was. Your wedding looked really lovely."

"When did you see pictures?"

"They were in the paper. That's when I decided to leave London."

"When did you meet Jean-Paul?"

She flushed again and looked away from him. "I've known Jean-Paul almost as long as I've known you. He owns a gallery in Paris."

It was the guilty expression in her eyes that suggested there was more to her relationship with the gallery owner than she was saying. Kane had always been jealous of the man who'd become her lover after him, always been insane at the fact that she'd carry another man's child so quickly. He'd been keenly aware that Jean-Paul had suited her artist's lifestyle more than a financier had.

"Did you see him at the same time you and I were together?"

"Would that upset you, Kane? It would be a bit hypocritical."

"Hypocritical or not, it pisses me off."

She smiled at him, her hands framing his face and pulling him close for a kiss. Her breath tasted of the sweet wine she'd had with dinner.

"My discomfort makes you happy?"

"Of course not. But I do like the fact that you care enough to be jealous."

If she only knew how possessive his thoughts about her were.

"I didn't date him when you and I were together. In fact, I never looked at another man."

An embarrassing relief flashed through him and he held her closer in his arms. "What has upset you tonight?"

She jerked away and unsettled her balance in the process. He saved her from falling to the floor and stood with her securely in his arms, walking to the living room and the large couch. He sat, still holding her loosely.

"Tell me."

"Why do you think something has upset me?"

"You're not a big drinker, Mary-Belle. And I've seen you like this only twice before."

She turned to press her face against his neck. "I don't want to think about it tonight. I want one perfect night with you."

"And you had to get drunk to enjoy it?"

"No. Getting drunk wasn't part of the plan. Just wanted to forget my troubles for a while. Just…enjoy being with you. Just…forget…everything."

With that she drifted to sleep in his arms. He held her that way for a long time, wondering what part he'd played in her upset. Regardless, he knew that tomorrow he'd have the answers he sought. But tonight he had Mary, even if this wasn't how he'd envisioned spending their first night together again.

Six

Mary groaned as she came awake, remembering drinking a little too much last night. She'd probably also said a bunch of stupid things. She rubbed her hand over her eyes at the thought. Suddenly she realized that she wasn't alone in bed. Kane's warm body was pressed along the back of hers, his arm around her waist anchoring her to him.

This was exactly where she'd wanted to end up, but she'd had a different path to get there in mind. She wished she remembered more of how they'd gotten into bed. She vaguely recalled Kane's questions before she'd fallen asleep on him. Before her mind could reconstruct more of the puzzle of the evening, she felt Kane caress her bare stomach.

She glanced down and saw that the old university T-shirt she wore was bunched up under her breasts. Kane's large hand spanned her entire stomach, his fingers moving in a pattern over her skin. His little finger rested a scant inch from the top of her midnight-blue thong.

She groaned, closing her eyes. She didn't want to see his hands on her. Didn't want to remember the way it felt when he made love to her first thing in the morning with the early light of day spilling through the windows.

The panic that Channing had inspired in her last night had faded away. She wasn't running from her cousins. And she wasn't going to run from Kane.

The past week had proven that Kane was sincere in wanting to be in her life. And she was ready to acknowledge that she wanted him there. More importantly, she wanted him in her bed.

Being his mistress wasn't an option this time—Kane had said as much. But marriage… There was too much history between them for her to even contemplate it.

With her eyes closed, her other senses went on high alert. All her analyzing stopped. Kane's scent and his warmth surrounded her. Damn, he was so hot pressed against her back. She tried to stay still, but when his hand edged up under the cotton shirt and brushed the underside of her breast, she shifted against him thrusting herself against his hand.

He cupped her, his forefinger caressing a circle around her nipple. Her nipple tightened and her breast felt fuller, but no matter how she moved, Kane kept his touch away from where she wanted it the most.

He urged her onto her back, staying on his side so that he was leaning over her, his warm hand still holding her breast. She couldn't think as his fingers moved over her, teasing her areola until she grabbed his wrist and dragged his palm over her nipple, creating the sensation she desired. She rubbed against his hand, closing her eyes and moaning softly.

He drew his hand away and she opened her eyes, fighting not to beg him for what she wanted. But Kane had always been a dominant lover. One who demanded everything she had to give.

"Please," she whispered finally, unable to resist another moment.

"Please what, Mary-Belle?"

"Please touch me."

"I am."

"My nipple."

"I did."

"With your mouth, Kane."

He lowered his head and his mouth settled over her extended nipple through the cotton T-shirt. The wet warmth made her hips arch off the bed.

She buried her hands in his hair. "More."

He lifted his head and stared down at her. "What?"

"I want more, please."

"Over here?" he asked, lowering his head over her other nipple. The air cooled the now exposed wet fabric, garnering an erotic shiver.

Her hips moved again. She wanted more. She *needed* more. "Suckle me."

He sucked stronger at her breast and his hand settled over her other nipple, caressing. She felt the exquisitely delicious pinch of his fingers against one nipple as his teeth bit gently at the other breast. The combined sensation made moisture pool between her legs.

She grabbed for his hips, trying to drag him over her, desperately needing to feel him pressed to her entire body. Now.

"Kane..."

He hummed against her breast, and the sound vibrated against her sensitized skin. She shifted her legs, encountering his hairy leg pressed next to hers on the bed.

She tried again to pull him over her, but he moved his hand from her breast to her stomach and lifted his head. She stared up at him. Her body on fire and that need, she knew, would be clearly in her eyes.

It had been so long since she'd made love. Kane had been her only lover, and fantasies of having him in her bed had sustained her through her long celibacy.

"What do you want, my sweet?"

"I want you over me. Now. I want to feel you

between my legs and against my belly. I need you, Kane."

She swept her hands down his body, pushing her hand through the opening in the front of his boxers and caressing the length of his erection, then lower to cup his sac in her hands. She rolled his balls together, teasing him with her nails on his sensitive skin.

She felt a drop of moisture on the tip of his erection and rubbed her fingers over it, smoothing it down the length of him. He never closed his eyes, never let his control slip.

Finally he grasped her wrist. "Take off your shirt."

As soon as he let go of her hand she did as he'd ordered, pulling the T-shirt up her body and tossing it on the floor.

She glanced down at her breasts and saw her nipples were hard and red. She sighed as Kane rubbed his forefinger over each of them before sliding his hand lower on her stomach.

"Take off your panties."

She pushed them down her legs and then kicked them aside. Now she lay under his gaze completely bare and she remembered the small changes in her body—the ones that time and life had put there. Until this moment, she hadn't considered how vulnerable she would feel.

Before she could cover herself, Kane lowered his head, taking her mouth in a slow kiss that made her insecurities disappear and focused her attention on the fire that he'd started in her.

When he lifted his head, he said, "Remove my boxers."

She nodded and reached for the fabric, but it was hard to do lying on her back, so she shifted to her knees, pushing him onto his back, slowly drawing the fabric over his erection and down his legs. She tossed the last item of clothing on the floor.

She stayed on her knees next to his hips, her fingers caressing his jutting erection. She took her time exploring his length and hardness. His legs shifted apart and she reached between them to cup his sac once again, then slid her touch lower to press against the flesh between his legs, and his hips lifted from the bed.

"No more of that. Are you on the pill?"

"Yes," she said.

"Thank God."

She laughed at the relief in his voice. "You wouldn't wear a condom for me."

"I would, but I enjoy the feel of your heat so much. Part your legs for me."

She did and he slid one finger through the curls at the juncture of her thighs, pushing it into her body, drawing out her moisture and smiling up at her as he used that moisture to lubricate his erection.

"Come here and straddle me," he said.

She did, loving the feel of his big, strong body

under hers. She rubbed her wetness over his erection, not letting him enter her body, just teasing both of them with the anticipation of being so close to one another. She leaned down, rubbing her breasts against his chest and brushing her lips against his neck.

His hands caressed her back, sliding down to her hips, where he spread her legs apart and slipped his shaft against her opening. "Sit up. Take me into your body."

"I want to feel your arms around me," she said.

As soon as the words slipped out she realized she'd said them out loud and that she'd revealed too much. But he only reversed their positions on the bed.

"Watch me take you, Mary. Know that I'm staking my claim on you again."

She swallowed but did as he'd asked, watched him open her body with two fingers and push the broad head of his penis against her. With just the tip nestled inside her body, he grabbed her hips, anchoring her to him as he thrust deep, sliding all the way home. He wrapped his arms around her back and pulled her into his chest as his hips plunged in and out. Driving her to the pinnacle, he held her with one arm, the other hand going between their bodies to stroke her and drive her over the edge before him.

Everything in her body tightened and she felt her orgasm wash over her. But she didn't slide down into dreamy relaxation. Instead Kane's rhythm drove her again to the edge of a climax, his hands holding her head and forcing her gaze to his. He took them both to the edge of their orgasms and held them there.

Finally she couldn't take it anymore. Scoring her nails down his body, she ran her finger along his butt and then lower, pressing against his flesh. She heard him curse her name and jerk against her as he spilled himself inside her. Her climax followed his.

She held him tightly in her arms as he collapsed on her, crushing her to the bed with his weight as they both slowly came back to earth.

He lifted his head. "Good morning."

She pulled his head to hers and their mouths met. Keeping her eyes open, she watched the intensity in his dark gaze sharpen as he kissed her. His mouth moved on hers in a slow, unhurried way, as if he had all day to explore.

He shifted, taking most of his weight on his elbows. His hips still nestled between her legs, his chest brushed her breasts.

He rubbed his mouth over hers, cradling her head in his hands. She smoothed her hands from his neck down to his arms. He was so strong as he held himself over her. She tightened her fingers on his muscles. He had the kind of strength, inside and out, that she'd always wanted.

When she lay in his arms she felt safe, protected and not alone. From the very beginning it had been that way.

He lifted his head expanding the intimacy between

them and their breath mingled. She tried to smile at him, to keep him from guessing how confused she was inside.

Kane closed his arms possessively around Mary, rolling to his back and taking her with him. No other woman had ever affected him the way she did. He wanted her—Mary—and no one else. Now that he had her in his bed, he vowed he'd never let her go again.

He wanted to spend the day here, with her between these sheets. He mentally reviewed his schedule and knew that he was going to piss off a lot of people when he canceled his morning meetings.

Mary snuggled into him, and he shut his eyes as a rush of emotion swamped him. Uncomfortable with the strength of his feelings for her, he crushed her to him, holding on. She embraced him with all the strength in her woman's body.

Kane felt a shift deep inside, something that he'd been afraid to let himself feel before. In fact, he wasn't too damned sure he liked it. But life had proven that Mary was the only woman for him. He wasn't prepared to share the emotion with her, but he planned to keep her by his side forever.

He'd use sex and her dependence on his financial knowledge to bind her to him. He'd use whatever it took to tie her to him in so many ways she wouldn't be able to leave him.

He caressed her entire body, loving the softness

of her skin. He'd missed the freedom to reach out and touch her. Over the past week, when they'd spent long hours working in her office, he'd wanted to touch her so many times. But always he'd been very aware that the privilege hadn't been his. Through his own decisions, he'd given up that right.

But he had it back now and he intended to keep it.

She moved against him and he slid his thigh between hers. She angled her face close, brushing her lips along his, tangling her tongue with his. He nibbled at her jaw, dropping kisses down the side of her neck. She had beard burn on her neck, and he felt a surge of possessiveness that he'd marked her as his own, that there was physical evidence that she'd given her sweet body to him.

He suckled at the skin in the valley between her breasts, leaving another mark. A private one visible to just the two of them.

"You're mine."

She froze and he realized he'd spoken out loud. The possessiveness he felt had spilled over in his words and tone. But he didn't regret them. One of the mistakes he'd made last time had been thinking he could control the force of his feelings for Mary by allocating her to the role of mistress. It hadn't worked and he'd ended up hurting both of them in the process. This time things would be different.

He stared at her. "Aren't you?"

She didn't close her eyes or flinch away from his

gaze, and he could only hope the rawness of what he felt wasn't revealed there. She cupped his jaw in her hands, her long artist's fingers cold against his skin. He waited, even as he wanted to demand she admit she was his.

"Mary?" So much for patience. Where she was concerned, he had none. Too much time had been wasted already.

"Yes. I'm yours. And you're mine. No one else's but mine."

"Damn straight," he said, stroking his hands down her body and sliding between her legs. He drove into her body, felt her flinch as he thrust himself into her while she was still too sensitive and not yet ready for him.

But she didn't push him away. She took him deep, welcomed him into her embrace even though he was hurting her.

Mary was the only person who made him forget the civilized man he was. He cursed, holding himself still.

"I'm sorry."

She soothed him with her caressing hand and held him to her breast. "For what? You didn't hurt me. I was only surprised."

Despite her assurances, he knew that he had. He suckled her pretty breasts and felt her tighten around his erection. He scraped his teeth along her sensitive skin, building the fire again with his kisses and his touch, drawing her along with him. When her hips moved under his, he started thrusting deep into her body. That manic need for her tingled at the back of his spine. He needed more of her. He needed to leave his mark so deep inside her that she'd never forget she belonged to him.

He pushed her thighs farther apart, put his arms under her legs until they were draped over them, granting him more intense access.

She gasped his name. The sound made his balls tighten, then his climax was upon him and he shouted her name, held her under him while he rode out his orgasm. Her muscles contracted around his body, cresting the waves of her own fulfillment.

He settled onto his side, tugging her into his arms. He didn't know if he would ever be sated. Everything about her fueled his passion and made him desire her more. But he didn't want their relationship to be all about sex. He needed to continue to show her that he wanted more than her body.

She shifted in his embrace. "I have a meeting this morning."

He swept his hands down her back and anchored her more fully against him. "Skip it."

She tipped her head back to frown at him. "I'm not your mistress anymore, Kane."

"I didn't think you were."

"I can't skip my meeting because you want to spend the day in bed. I have responsibilities."

"I realize that. It's not as if I'm not planning to rearrange my day to spend it with you."

"I can't do that."

"Can't or won't?"

"Won't," she said, closing her eyes. "It would be so easy to do this. To stay here with you all day and pretend that the outside world doesn't exist. But it's waiting for me when I go home. And putting it off isn't going to make anything better."

"What are you so afraid of?" he asked. Mary had never been one to really deal with her problems. She abandoned them. She'd run away more than once, and he knew she'd do it again if she had to.

"What makes you think I'm afraid of anything?" she asked in a silky tone that told him he was treading on thin ice.

"You were drinking heavily last night—it's usually a sign."

She pushed against his chest. He knew she wanted out of his arms—not to mention his bed—and for a minute he refused to let he go. He knew once he did that she'd put barriers between them.

"Kane, let me go."

He relaxed his hold and watched her slip from the bed. She bent to pick up his T-shirt from the floor and he couldn't help admiring the curve of her backside. She glanced over her shoulder at him, catching him eyeing her.

She smiled unexpectedly. "Later we can spend time together. I'm free this weekend…all weekend."

Kane rubbed the back of his neck. Part of him hated being in a relationship that included compromise, but he knew that Mary wasn't going to change her mind. "I have to wait four days to make love to you again?"

"No. Only four days to spend all day naked together."

"Okay. I have meetings that I really shouldn't rearrange—one of the men I'm meeting with flew out from L.A. last night." Bill Hutchins was here for an interview. A top-notch finance whiz kid who Kane had spent more than three months trying to convince that working for Brentwood Investments would be his dream job.

"But you would have postponed for me?" she asked.

He would move the world for her if he could. She was his obsession, and it was only now, more than ten years after the first time they'd met, that he acknowledged that fact to himself.

"Yes." Even as he said it, he felt a twinge of anxiety at the feelings that one word evoked. Under the weight of her stare he stalked into the bathroom, knowing that he was attempting to run from emotions that he couldn't escape.

Seven

Kane was withdrawn as they left his house. Mary had walked over last night and he'd insisted on driving her home this morning. She'd already called Max to let him know she'd be late for their meeting.

She knew she was to blame for this awkwardness between her and Kane. When he'd walked away from her in the bedroom she'd understood that she had the power to hurt Kane in ways she'd never contemplated before. And she never wanted to do that to him.

"Thanks for driving me home," she said, enjoying the feel of the wind on her face as they rode in Kane's Jaguar convertible. It was a pretty lame thing to say, but she'd never been good at being tentative.

Breaking the ice had always been something she'd done by being…well, herself. In the old days she would have put her hands between his legs and kissed him hard on the mouth. That action would have shocked him out of his sulk. But having insisted they not focus solely on their sexual relationship, she couldn't use that technique.

"No problem," he said, keeping his eyes on the road and his tone curt.

She watched the scenery pass for a few minutes. She didn't want to start her day with this coldness between them. She wasn't exactly sure how it had happened, but Kane had become her calm oasis in a life that was a chaotic mess and she didn't want to give that up. "I'm sorry I wouldn't—"

"Don't. This isn't about you."

She couldn't have felt worse if he'd slapped her. She withdrew, though her first instinct was to lash out at him, to start the kind of fight she would have in the past. But she wasn't that woman any longer.

She looked at him, at that aristocratic profile, and felt the loud, argumentative words bubbling up inside of her. She tightened her hands into fists, digging her fingernails into her palms.

He pulled into her driveway and entered the code to open the large metal gates that had protected the privacy of the Duvall family for years. As soon as they were beyond the gates, he stopped the car, putting it in Park.

He turned to face her, taking her hands in his own. Opening them gently, he smoothed the crescent marks her nails had made with a brush of his lips.

"What are you hiding?" he asked against her palm.

She shuddered and tried to focus on what he was saying and not what he was doing. That tenderness made her want to bare her soul and tell him the secrets that were her constant companions—the ones that were going to drive a wedge between them the longer she kept silent.

"Mary-Belle?"

"My temper," she admitted. "I'm not doing a very good job of it."

"You don't have to hide it from me," he said, meeting her gaze squarely.

"Yes, I do. I have to remember to keep in control at all times. Ladies don't have outbursts like spoiled children." There were more rules running through the back of her mind like a litany. She heard her mother's voice more frequently now that she was struggling to be the dutiful daughter. The voice was the same stringent one that Mary remembered from childhood.

"Your passionate nature is a part of who you are," Kane said. "Is that why you don't paint anymore?"

She didn't want to talk about her painting. It had been her salvation on the path back to the land of the living. She had revealed more of herself in her latest pieces than she'd wanted to, but the canvas was the only place she had left to be herself. "I'm not really passionate—not anymore."

He shook his head. "Yes, you are. I still catch glimpses of that fervor you always had. No matter how hard you try to hide it, it's there."

"Please don't say things like that. My life is about decorum now. If you think you see passion, ignore it."

"I don't think I can."

"Kane, I'm serious. Don't encourage me to be the way I used to be. I'm weak and—"

"Good, I like you weak. I'm sorry I was an ass before. I'm sulking because I didn't get my way."

"No problem. I don't necessarily like being the conscientious one."

"But you will be."

She *had* to be. Kane would never understand how far she'd fallen after her baby's death. How depressed she'd been and how outrageously she'd acted. *He* may have seen her drink too much only two other times, but he hadn't seen the excesses she'd gone to in Paris after her son died. Kane hadn't seen the way she'd ceased to be the woman he'd known.

The woman she was today was a carefully pieced together version of herself. She sometimes felt like Humpty Dumpty with a fragile eggshell that wasn't going to hold. She feared the cracks left when she'd reassembled her life would gape open and show the vulnerable woman underneath.

"I'm trying to figure out this new you. Each time

I get close I see something else that doesn't fit, a new piece of the puzzle."

"Please don't. You see more clearly than anyone, and right now I'm not ready for that. I don't want to be naked with you when I feel this way."

"We have to move forward, darling. No matter what scars you think you carry, I won't shy away from them."

She wished those words were true. But there was so much of her that Kane didn't know. Too many secrets that were threatening to expose themselves under her cousins' prying eyes.

"Please just drop me off at the house. We can talk about this later."

"If that's what you want."

"It is."

He put the car in gear and didn't say anything again until they'd reached the circular drive in front of her house. He reached over, put his hand on the back of her neck and drew her near to take her mouth in a kiss that left no doubt about the passion he felt for her.

"I told you she couldn't help herself."

Lorette's voice was like a glass of ice water being dumped on Mary. She guiltily pulled away from Kane and turned to face her cousins and their lawyer.

Kane was seriously beginning to dislike Mary's cousins. He watched Mary start to speak and then close her eyes to count quietly, once again battling to maintain her ladylike facade. He also was beginning to really hate that counting thing she did.

"There's nothing scandalous in a man kissing his fiancée," Kane said, pushing open his door and getting out of the car.

"You're engaged?" Lorette asked. The incredulity on her face made Kane's smile deepen.

"Yes. Mary has just now agreed to be my wife."

Mary stared at him with a wildness in her eyes that told him she was going to lose her control in a few seconds. As much as he wanted to see her drop her guard, he knew that she would regret doing so in front of her cousins.

He squeezed her shoulder reassuringly before opening her door and assisting her out of the Jaguar. He leaned down to kiss her again because he knew that this was the right decision. Why hadn't he thought of it before now? His ring on her finger was exactly what he wanted.

Carmen stood in the doorway as Kane glanced up. "Carmen, we're going to need a bottle of champagne on the terrace to celebrate."

"Right away, sir."

Kane put his arm around Mary, tucking her under his shoulder and walking up the front steps past her cousins.

He stopped in front of the third person, a man he didn't know. "I'm afraid we haven't been introduced."

"This is Max Previn. Max, this is Kane Brentwood."

Kane held his hand out to the other man, who shook it firmly. "Are you one of Mary's relatives?"

"No, I'm the Duvall family lawyer. Lorette and Channing were concerned when Mary didn't make our meeting this morning."

"I'm sorry, Max. Didn't your assistant relay my message to you?"

"He just did. But we were already here."

"Carmen told us you've been out all night," Channing said.

Mary flushed, and Kane refused to act as though they'd done anything wrong. This wasn't the Dark Ages. They were adults in an adult relationship.

"That was my fault," he said to Max, ignoring Channing completely because otherwise he'd succumb to the urge to punch the other man. "I knew Mary had an appointment, but I wouldn't let her leave my house until she agreed to marry me."

Max smiled at them and Mary cleared her throat. "Kane, I need to speak to you—privately."

"Certainly, darling," he said, smiling at her. "We'll join all of you on the terrace in a few minutes to toast our engagement."

Kane followed Mary to the study. He leaned against the door after closing it. She turned to him, and he saw the Mary he remembered flashing in those Caribbean-blue eyes of hers.

"What the hell are you thinking? You can't say outrageous things like that in front of them. They are already suspicious of our relationship. Pretending to be engaged isn't going to help matters."

"I'm not pretending. We are engaged."

"Really? I must have missed something, because I don't remember you asking me to marry you."

"Your cousins forced my hand."

"You really want us to get married?" she asked.

"Yes, I really do. I hadn't thought of marriage this soon because I know that I need to rebuild the trust between us. But your cousins are a pain in the ass, and I think an engagement will shut them up."

"I don't want you to marry me to keep my cousins off my back."

He realized that Mary did want to be his wife despite her protests. But he was very close to saying the wrong thing and driving her away from him. He knew he had to handle this carefully and, as always when he was around Mary, his usual eloquence deserted him.

He wanted to order her to marry him. He wanted her to agree and then have her do it. But that wasn't going to happen anytime in this century.

"Mary, tonight I'll ask you properly."

"I can't go out there and lie to them."

"I'm not asking you to lie to them. I want the chance to ask you to be my wife properly."

"Well, I'm not sure I'm going to say yes."

"You said that you were mine," he reminded her, pacing toward her.

She retreated until she collided with the desk and had to stop. He kept walking until only an inch of space was between them. He put his hands on her hips and closed the space.

Lowering his mouth, he kissed her, slowly pouring everything he felt for her into it. He tried to convey his apologies for all the mistakes and missteps he'd taken since the moment they'd met.

"I'm not taking no for an answer. You can either agree to be my wife or I'm going out there and telling your cousins that you were once my mistress."

"Blackmail? Isn't that below you?"

"I'll stop at nothing to make you mine. It's what I should have done the first time I saw you, but I was too overwhelmed by what you made me feel."

"I— Okay, Kane. I'll marry you."

Kane left shortly after Mary agreed to marry him and they'd had their champagne toast. He promised her he'd be back at six for dinner. Lorette and Channing departed with Max a few minutes later. Mary had told them that she'd known Kane when she lived in Europe but that their affair had ended before she'd returned home. Another half-truth that she hoped would appease them.

After that confrontation she felt stretched beyond the limits of her self-control, so she escaped to the small studio her grandfather had had made for her. She locked the door behind her and stripped off the slightly rumpled dress from the previous evening until she was completely naked. She stood still for a minute, breathing in the unaccustomed sensation of freedom. Slowly, the proper-society layers fell away, leaving her feeling more like her true self. She found the brightly colored skirt that she'd hidden in the wardrobe and donned it. Then she pulled out a bright red button-down shirt and knotted the tail ends under her breasts. The transformation was complete.

She stared at the canvas she'd been working on in secret for the last few nights. Though she was best known for her lush landscapes, this piece was a portrait started after Kane had reentered her life. Her guilt and chaotic thoughts faded as she immersed herself in her painting. A sudden knock on the door interrupted her. She grabbed a smock from the hook on the wall to cover her clothing, then unlocked the door, opening it a crack.

"Yes, Carmen?"

"You have guests on the terrace."

"Who?" she asked, not sure she could face Channing and Lorette one more time today.

"Emma Dearborn and Lily Cartwright."

She couldn't send her friends away. As cathartic as her painting was, her friends would boost her spirits. "I'll be down in a few minutes. I have to clean up."

"I'll let them know."

Mary waited until she heard Carmen's footsteps fade, then left the studio, taking care to lock the door behind her. She hurried to her bedroom, where she washed up as quickly as possible and changed into a very proper Ann Taylor sundress. Without time to return to the studio, she tucked her painting clothes in the bottom drawer of her dresser.

She was halfway down the stairs before she remembered she wasn't wearing shoes and ran back up to find some sandals. Finally she made it to the terrace to find her friends relaxing on the Adirondack chairs, soaking up the sun. Each wore sunglasses and held a glass of Carmen's ice-cold lemonade in her hand.

"Hey, there. Sorry to keep you waiting. So to what do I owe the surprise visit?" Mary asked.

"We're on rumor patrol," Lily said, pulling her sunglasses down her nose to stare at Mary.

"Rumor patrol?" Mary asked, feeling a sinking in the pit of her stomach. What had they heard? Had news of her being Kane's mistress leaked out? Or was the fact that she'd had a child in Paris now part of the Eastwick gossip mill? She fumbled for the sunglasses she held in her hand and put them on.

Emma tipped her head to one side. "Yes. Why did we have to hear from Lorette that you are engaged to your gorgeous English guy?"

Oh, the engagement. "Well, they were here when Kane brought me home this morning."

"You spent the night with him? Are we going to get the juicy details?" Lily said, waggling her eyebrows at Mary.

"No, you're not." Mary shook her head and laughed. This kind of silliness was just what she needed. Her friends gave her space to be herself. It was one of the aspects of her new life that she really loved—her renewed friendship with the Debs.

Carmen had left a pitcher of lemonade on the table, so Mary poured herself a glass, then sank into the chair next to Emma.

"Come on, Mary. It's not fair to be so close-mouthed about him. We knew something was up as soon as you fainted into his arms," Lily said.

"I didn't faint into his arms," Mary protested.

"Yes, you did. It was very…un-Marylike. Why did you faint like that?" Emma asked.

Mary was too tired of the all the lies and half-truths she was keeping to make up stories for her friends. "I never thought I'd see him again. I don't know why I passed out, though. I must have looked like an idiot."

Lily reached around Emma to squeeze Mary's hand. "I thought it looked very romantic. He practically ran across the room to catch you."

Mary had known from the moment she'd opened her eyes and felt his arms around her that something had changed between them.

"I bet he was planning to ask you to marry him from that moment," Emma said.

"I don't know."

"So where's the ring?" Lily asked.

"I don't have one."

"Why not?" Emma looked slightly indignant.

Yes, Mary, why not? "Well, um, he's going to ask me properly tonight."

"Properly? How'd he ask you the first time?"

She couldn't tell them that he'd simply announced she'd marry him in front of her cousins. That proposal hardly matched the romantic vision her friends were spinning. Plus it might open a topic of conversation she didn't want to pursue at the moment. "None of your business."

"Ooh, I bet it was a sexy proposal…maybe in his bedroom?" Once again, Lily waggled her eyebrows, clearly hoping for some of those *juicy details* she'd asked about earlier.

"I'm not telling," Mary said, blushing even though she shouldn't be.

Fortunately she distracted her friends with a different discussion. They stayed another thirty minutes, catching up with everything going on in their lives. Mary said goodbye with promises to share the real proposal when it happened. As she watched them drive away, she knew yet another reason to value the Debs—in their presence, she didn't feel like a fraud.

Eight

Kane rarely felt nervous. But he was tonight. He wanted every detail to be perfect, down to the flowers decorating the room.

While he'd convinced Mary to be his fiancée in front of her family and lawyer, he still had his work cut out for him. She wasn't going to marry him unless he could convince her their relationship was the real thing and not a charade.

He'd rescheduled his meetings after leaving Mary earlier because business seemed insignificant compared to the more pressing task at hand—finding the right ring for her. He'd known exactly the ring he wanted; it had been locating it that proved to be the challenge.

He reached into his pocket to ensure the box was still there. He straightened his tie and took one last run through his house. His staff had followed his orders to the letter. Fresh-cut flowers adorned every surface, candles flickered in every room. The hall to the bedroom had been strewn with rose petals and the room itself had been transformed into the ultimate romantic fantasy.

Or at least Mary's romantic fantasy. He knew she liked lush, vibrant material and had a bit of a sheikh fetish. So he'd created a luxurious room worthy of the most arrogant sheikh and his favorite harem girl with candles, pillows and draped fabric.

He stopped in the kitchen to check the last-minute details with his chef before leaving to pick up Mary.

The September evening was cool but comfortable, so he left the top down on his convertible, knowing Mary enjoyed open-air rides. When he arrived at the Duvall mansion, he rang the doorbell and was pleasantly surprised that Mary answered the door.

She wore one of those oh so proper dresses that seemed to fill her current wardrobe. This one was slim-fitting, demurely cut and sleeveless. She looked elegant and poised, although the way she fiddled with the strand of pearls betrayed her nervousness.

"Good evening," he said, taking her hand and dropping a kiss on the back of it.

"Hello, Kane. You look very nice."

He arched one eyebrow at her. "Glad you noticed. You look beautiful as always."

He put his hand at the small of her back to escort her to the car and encountered silky bare skin. He paused as Mary walked in front of him and he admired the daring cut of the dress. The elegant curve of her spine was revealed by the fabric that started right about her buttocks.

"That dress should be illegal," he muttered as he opened the passenger door for her.

"I don't know what you're talking about. It is really demure."

"From the front you look respectable. But the back is pure temptation."

She tipped her head to the side, her eyes twinkling with mischief. "I'm glad."

"Tease."

She just smiled at him as he slipped behind the wheel of the car and roared down her driveway onto the street. That feeling of rightness that Mary always inspired in him swelled to include this place—Eastwick, Connecticut. He knew that he was going to make this town his home—all because of the complicated woman sitting next to him.

"How was your day?" he asked, reaching over to take her hand in his, holding it loosely on his thigh.

"Weird."

"Weird?"

"Yes. This morning some crazy man told me I was going to marry him, my cousins actually left me alone, and I spent time with a couple of my friends."

"That doesn't sound weird to me."

"It wouldn't. You're the crazy man."

"Do you really think it's so crazy to want to marry the woman who sets my body on fire and makes my life fuller?"

"I make your life fuller?" she asked in a soft tentative voice.

"In ways you'll never understand."

"Maybe you're not crazy."

He laughed because he knew she wanted him to, but he couldn't help the niggling worry that sprang to life. Was she feeling pressured to marry him? Working hard to achieve his goals wasn't something he'd ever balked at, but he was realizing that Mary wouldn't always fall into his plans just because he wanted her to. She was going to take all of his concentration.

"What about you—did you have a productive day?"

"No," he said. "You distracted me."

"How did I do that?"

"By agreeing to marry me."

"Really?"

He gave her a measuring look. She knew he didn't make things up.

"Silly question. It's just so hard to imagine you letting something—anything—interfere with business."

He didn't like what that said about the man who Mary had let be her lover in London. She must have felt as though she was a convenience and segregated to only one part of his life. Though he'd certainly acted that way, the opposite had been true.

Then, he'd had to fight the urge to rush to her flat several times a day. He'd forced himself to never visit her more than three times a week. It had been difficult, but she'd been his mistress and he'd thought it necessary to keep the boundaries firmly in place.

"I'm not that man any longer," he said, pulling into his own driveway and braking in front of the house. "And you're not my mistress, Mary. You are the woman who is going to spend the rest of her life with me."

"Convince me this isn't just one more error in judgment on my part," she said.

"I intend to."

As Kane led her to the terrace off his living room, Mary noticed he'd put a lot of planning into setting the stage for the evening. She was almost afraid to believe his marriage offer had been sincere and not motivated by the wish to protect her.

Why now? The question—or some variation of it—had been going through her mind since the moment Kane had come back into her life. Why was he determined that this time they have a relationship and not an arrangement?

"Would you like a martini?" Kane asked from the door.

"I think I'll pass. I don't want to repeat last night."

Kane smiled as he pulled her into his arms, swaying to the smooth sounds of Sade pouring from the speakers.

"Do you remember the first time we danced together?" he asked, his words a breathy whisper spoken right into her ear.

She did remember. This song, "Diamond Lies," had been playing. She'd been incredibly nervous as it had been her first outing with Kane. Her years growing up in Eastwick had proven that she was horribly inept in any social gathering. But on Kane's arm, all her awkwardness had disappeared. She'd felt beautiful and confident wearing a tasteful but very sexy dress he'd purchased for her.

That night had changed the way she viewed herself. After that, her confidence in herself had started to build.

She rested her head against his shoulder now as his hands roamed along her back to settle low on her hips. Kane was a superb dancer, and she'd always loved going clubbing with him.

"I remember this song," she said. Kane had flown her to a Sade concert for her birthday one year. After the concert he'd given her a stunning diamond-and-sapphire choker, which he'd insisted be the only thing she wore when they went to bed. They'd spent the rest of the weekend making love in their luxurious hotel suite.

The song ended and blended into "Let's Get It On" by Marvin Gaye. She leaned her head back, resting her hands on his lapels. "Not very subtle."

"That one was supposed to come on later," he said, looking chagrined. But his grip on her hips shifted as he canted his hips forward so that his hard-on nudged her lower stomach.

"How much later?" she asked, going up on tiptoe and rubbing her lips over his until his mouth opened and she slipped her tongue inside.

His hand came up to hold the back of her neck, angling her head and taking control of the kiss. He tangled his tongue with hers and kissed her with a thoroughness that left her aching for him.

"After dinner," he said, leaning away and setting her from him.

She didn't want to wait until after dinner. Her breasts felt too full, her skin was flushed and too sensitive, and moisture pooled low in her body. "Will the meal be ruined if we delay it an hour or so?"

"No, but my proposal won't go as planned," he said, cupping her face and kissing her again. She held on to his arms, anchoring herself to this man who had become the center of her world again. Before they lost control, he firmly stepped away to lean against the railing, looking out over the water.

"What do you have planned?" she asked, taking

deep breaths and getting her body back in check. Trying to appear as composed as Kane did, she walked over to stand next to him.

"A surprise," he said, pulling a remote from his pocket and switching CDs. "We'll save Marvin for later. Have you walked through the gardens here?"

"Not since I was a little girl. The Olsteins owned this place then and they had a boy my brother's age. I attended a few birthday parties for him."

"You never talk much about your brother. What was he like?"

She hadn't thought of Alex in years. He had been four years younger than her and cut from the perfect Duvall mold—unlike Mary. "Perfect, at least in my parents' eyes."

"What about in your eyes?"

"He was so cute when he was little. I didn't start to disappoint my mother and the family until I was twelve, so until then, Alex and I got along really well."

"I don't understand much about your relationship with your mother."

"Trust me, Kane, there's nothing to understand. We were complete opposites and she couldn't accept me for who I was. She wanted to have a perfect little model to promote her theories on ladylike child rearing. The memories chilled her. "I don't want to talk about her."

Seeming to accept her pronouncement, Kane escorted her into the garden, which had been draped with strands of clear lights. The entire space looked ethereal, like something from a dream.

"I want to know your family history," he said, proving that he wasn't entirely finished with the topic.

She had always sought to distance herself from her family as well as other people she'd never felt connected to because her very nature made them so dissimilar. But lately she'd recognized that there was more attachment between her and her family than she'd ever realized. Had her parents lived, would she have eventually found her way home to them? Although it was too late to know, the question niggled at her. "There's no one left except me and the cousins. What about you?"

Enough talking about her and relationships that couldn't be changed. She'd have to live forever with the knowledge that her parents had died feeling that she was a failure to them.

"I severed all ties with my family when I made the decision to annul my marriage to Victoria."

"Is there any chance of a reconciliation with them?"

"I doubt it."

Mary heard the finality in his voice. A note of fear entered her being. She sensed that Kane had felt betrayed by his family and their unwillingness to support him in the dissolution of his marriage. Something he could never forgive.

So how would he accept the fact that she'd lied about being pregnant with another man's child?

* * *

Kane wished they'd never started talking about their families and was very glad that they'd arrived at the fountain in the center of the garden. It was the perfect place to propose to Mary.

He'd had a large padded seat cushion put down on the wrought iron bench. The lights gave the night a magical quality and, combined with the music, made him feel as though they had stepped beyond the boundaries of time. And that was how he felt about Mary—she was destined to be his…always.

He was a practical man by vocation and nature, but there was something about this woman that made him believe in things that couldn't be seen or proven. When they were together, something deep inside him felt right. Felt as if he was exactly where he was meant to be.

"You went through a lot of trouble putting this together," she said.

"It wasn't too bad."

"Um…there's something I should tell you before you ask me to marry you. Something about my marriage to Jean-Paul—"

"I don't want to hear it." The very last thing he wanted to discuss with Mary was her first husband. He hated the fact that another man had married her and given her a child and Kane wasn't prepared to be civilized about it.

She bit her lower lip. "I'm sorry."

"I should be a bigger man and more understanding about your ex-husband, but I'm not."

"That's okay, it's just that… Never mind. You're right, this is the wrong time. I should also apologize for what I said earlier—you know, that today was weird and calling you crazy."

She was nervous. He could tell by her inane conversation and the way she was trying to distract him. But he wouldn't let her. "You'll have to make it up to me later."

She arched one eyebrow at him, looking very haughty. "I will?"

"Yes, you will."

"In bed?"

"Yes." He knew exactly how he'd have her when she apologized again. Underneath him, her heels on his shoulders as he brought her to the edge of climax again and again until she was breathless and pleading with him.

"I can't wait," she said.

He skimmed his gaze down her body, noticing that her nipples pebbled simply by his looking at them. "Me either."

He led her to the bench to sit, then turned away to get himself back under control, feeling suddenly anxious. He'd planned what he would say, rehearsed it in his mind. This marriage was about more than their present relationship. It was about bringing closure to and rectifying the way things had ended between them.

He faced her and saw her sitting very properly on the bench—legs crossed at her ankles, hands loosely held together on her lap. She was heartbreakingly beautiful, and he felt a pressure to not only get this right tonight but also to ensure that he kept it right for the rest of their lives.

He cleared his throat. "Antoine de Saint-Exupery once wrote 'Life has taught us that love does not consist of gazing at each other but in looking outward together in the same direction.' Until I met you, Mary, his words seemed like a contrivance."

He took a few steps closer to her. "I've always believed that, as a man, I'd set the course of any relationship I had. I did that with you in London when we first met—made my demands and arranged things so that you could accommodate me. But I realized—" he went down on one knee in front of her, taking both her hands in his "—that I was only fooling myself. No matter how much I wanted to believe I was in control of you and my reactions to you…that wasn't the case."

"Oh, Kane—"

"Shh," he said, putting his fingers over her lips to silence her. "Let me have my say."

She kissed his fingers before he drew them away, then took his hand in hers, staring at him with wide eyes. He felt the import of what he was doing. He understood that he couldn't fail her again the way he had when he'd deserted her to marry Victoria. The deep emotions in Mary's eyes mirrored the ones residing inside his soul—feelings that he hoped he'd never have to name because they'd leave him feeling extremely vulnerable.

"Finding you again, single and alone like I am, made me realize..." He couldn't say that fate wanted them to be together. He'd sound like some kind of pansy even though he did feel that way. Mary was his and she always would be. "Made me realize how much I wanted you in my life."

He reached into his pocket and pulled out the jewelry box. "So I'm asking you to marry me, Mary. Not because your cousins might gossip about us if we don't. Not because my family will approve. But because I want to wake up next to you every day for the rest of my life."

He took out the ring and held it in one hand, hoping he hadn't made a hash of things. He felt unsure what the tears in her eyes meant. Hell, it couldn't be good.

But then she held out her left hand. "I will marry you. I, too, want to wake up next to you every day. I like the thought of spending my life with you, Kane."

He slipped the ring onto her finger and stood, drawing her to her feet with him. He embraced her, kissing her as if she'd just given him the world. Of course, she had.

Nine

Dinner was sumptuous and very romantic, served under the stars in the middle of the garden. The meal was one of her favorites—a seafood dish that was light but filling—which they'd had together every time they'd vacationed in Capri.

As soon as they finished eating, Kane led her to the terrace, where they danced under the stars to all of their favorite songs—both slow and fast tempo. When "Let's Get It On" played again, they were in each other's arms.

Kane held her tightly to him as they danced to the song, letting the lyrics and old memories surround them. His erection brushed against her with each bump of his hips. She smiled up at him.

"Thank you," she said, not sure that the words were enough, but they were all she had right now.

"For?" he asked, dropping kisses along her neck and letting his hands caress her entire body.

She caught his face between her hands and kissed him deeply, not pulling back until she'd done a thorough job of it. "Making this night something out of a dream."

"You're welcome. I intend to make every night we spend together this way."

She knew she should try again to tell him about Jean-Paul, to confess that she'd never married the other man. But this time she stopped for selfish reasons. She wanted this dream night with Kane to never end. She wanted to bask in the tenderness she saw in his eyes. She wanted to be the woman he thought she was, at least for tonight.

"I want to do the same for you," she said at last.

"You already do," he said, lifting her up, and carrying her down the hallway to his bedroom. A path of rose petals directed the way. She was touched again at how much effort he'd put into making this night memorable for her.

No one had ever done anything on this scale for her. The closest thing she could compare it to was her grandfather converting an unused bedroom in the Duvall mansion for her studio. Somehow, that didn't compare. Grandfather David had insisted she keep the door firmly locked and her artwork a secret.

Kane wasn't hiding her or telling her to hide their affection from the world. He was sharing her romantic dreams and fantasies…making them come true.

He set her on her feet outside the bedroom door. "Go inside and get changed. I'll be right back."

"Where are you going?"

"It's a surprise," he said, kissing her quickly on the mouth and walking away.

She opened the door to a room that had been completely done over. She stood on the threshold and felt tears burn the back of her eyes. He'd given her a romantic fantasy straight from her desires.

She entered and felt as if she'd stepped back in time. The room was covered in large pillows—one huge round one the size of a queen bed sat in the middle. It was piled with smaller pillows covered in satins, silks and velvets. Fabric draped from the ceiling to the walls, giving the impression of a tent.

On the edge of the round bed was a garment bag with her name stenciled on it, along with a small velvet pouch. She picked them up and went into the bathroom to change.

She opened the garment bag and saw midnight-blue satin pants and a matching top. Both pieces were adorned with gold coins that jingled when she removed the outfit from the bag.

The pants rode low on her hips, and the top fastened between her bare breasts with a small hook.

The love bite that Kane had left on her this morning was visible just above the fastening.

She opened the velvet bag and found the sapphire-and-diamond choker that she'd returned to him when he'd announced his engagement to another woman. Mary fastened it around her neck, then pulled out a good-size sapphire that she knew to wear in her navel. Using the jewelry adhesive that was also in the bag, she secured the gem in her belly button.

She turned the bag upside down and four other pieces fell out—gold-and-sapphire bracelets and anklets. She put them on, then twirled around in a circle, listening to the music her costume made as she moved.

She smoothed her hands down her body, swaying her hips to the sound of the music in her head. She let everything fall away except the sensual woman deep inside her.

There was a knock on the door as she draped the veil over her head, securing it with the gold circlet and then attaching the transparent fabric that covered her face from the eyes down.

"I'm ready for you, Mary." Kane's deep voice sent shivers coursing through her.

"I'll be right out."

Her overnight bag was sitting on the floor next to the vanity. She grabbed her makeup bag from inside and quickly lined her eyes with the dark eyeliner.

She was more than ready for him. She took one last look at herself in the mirror and felt a settling in her soul that said she was coming close to understanding who she was meant to be.

Her true self was someone in between the Duvalls' expectations and her rebellious nature. She realized that Kane gave her the freedom to be this woman—the one who liked to be outrageous in private.

And now she wanted to reward him for helping her feel that way. She opened the door and saw him reclining on the round bed, waiting for her.

Kane hit the play button on the CD remote as soon as Mary walked out of the bathroom. The music was slow and sensuous, a CD from the belly-dancing classes she'd taken, which he'd found when he'd cleaned out her London flat.

"Do you want me to dance for you?" she asked. Her demeanor had changed with her clothing—the swaying of her hips was more pronounced, and her arms moved with each step. The bracelets and anklets provided a trilling accent to each movement.

"Hell, yes."

She tossed her head and gave him a look that was meant to seduce—all the more enticing because of the partial covering of her face—and he felt it go straight through his body to his groin.

This moment had occupied his thoughts all day long. Getting through the proposal and the dinner had been a difficult thing, but he'd held onto his restraint and given her the romance that every woman wanted.

She paused in the middle of the room and he held his arms open. "Come to me."

"I thought you wanted me to dance."

"I just plain want you. This night is for you."

She took two steps closer to the bed. He glimpsed the love bite he'd left on her chest earlier and a flare of possessiveness swamped him. Suddenly, he didn't think he had the patience for a slow seduction. He wanted her in his arms, where she belonged. He needed to feel her silky bare limbs entwined with his.

"I want this night for us," she said, reaching behind her back for a moment before lifting her arms over her head and dancing toward him.

The rhythm of her hips made her pants slide lower with each step she took. She must have lowered the zipper in the back to accomplish it. He held his breath, his eyes fixated on the blue gem in her belly button as she undulated her stomach muscles.

Her pants slipped lower as she turned in a half circle. The zipper was open only partway, and he reached out to tug it the rest of the way down.

When she spun again, her pants slid off her body and she delicately stepped out of them. She continued to dance around him, and he watched her with his hand on his erection, stroking it and aching for her.

She toyed with that hook that fastened her top—the only thing keeping him from seeing her bare breasts. She unfastened it and turned rapidly, letting the fabric flare out to expose her in flashes, teasing them both with what she revealed.

She shrugged her shoulders and the top slid down her arms, catching on her bracelets. Another shimmy and she stood in front of him wearing only the veil and her jewelry.

He rose from the bed to go to her. "Dance with me."

"We're both naked."

She wrapped her arms around him and they moved together in a sensuous dance that took Kane to the edge of exploding. He maneuvered them to the bed and gently pushed her onto it.

Kane sank next to her. They were so compatible in bed that he could easily imagine them spending their married lives together in intimacy.

She kissed his thigh, and he shifted, so that he was lying next to her, his erection pressing against her hip.

He took her mouth with his and let his hands wander over her body, still amazed that she was here in his bedroom and in his arms. This time she would be his forever. He knew there were shadows between them that needed to be discussed, and he should have let her tell him whatever it was in her past that she'd wanted to share. Soon, he vowed, but not now.

Her hips undulated, her hands grasping at him, trying to pull him on top of her. "Are you in a hurry?"

She buried her face against his chest. "Yes. No. I don't know. I just want you so much."

He pushed her legs apart, thinking of the ties that

were attached to the bed. He reached between her legs to find her welcoming humid warmth, the evidence of her desire for him.

"I noticed."

"I'm glad. Are you going to do something about it?"

"Yes." He left her side and went to the foot of the bed, finding the velvet ribbon that was attached to the fabric cover of the mattress. He took her left foot in his hand, bending to kiss her ankle before tying the ribbon around it.

"Kane, what are you doing?"

"Something," he said, fastening her other ankle to the opposite side of the mattress so that her legs were spread far apart and her feminine flesh was exposed to him. He crouched between her legs and looked up at her body.

She lifted her hips, a silent invitation for him to do more than look at her. He picked up a handful of the rose petals that littered the floor and dropped them over her body, starting at her feet and working his way up until he covered her to the neck.

She shivered with awareness and her nipples tightened. He arranged the petals on each of her breasts so that her nipples were surrounded by the soft rose petals.

He licked each nipple until it tightened even more. Then he blew gently on the tips. She raked her nails down his back in response.

Her hand covered his. She sat up, displacing the petals on her breasts. She moved the petals on her stomach around until they accented the blue gem in her navel. "How's that?"

"You messed up your breasts," he said.

"That's okay. It gives you a reason to fondle me again."

He did just that, taking his time to fix the petals and draw her nipples out by sucking them. He moved each of the petals on her stomach, nibbling at every inch of bare skin before replacing the petals. Then he knelt between her thighs and looked down at her.

He picked up another handful of petals and dropped them over the dark curls between her legs. She swallowed, her hands shifting on the bed next to her hips.

"Open yourself for me," he said.

Her legs moved, but he took her hands in his, bringing them to her mound. She hesitated before she pulled those lower lips apart. The pink flesh looked so delicate and soft with the red rose petals around it.

"Hold still," he said.

He arranged the petals so that her delicate skin was centered. He blew lightly on her before tonguing that soft flesh. She lifted her hips and he drew her flesh into his mouth, carefully sucking on her. He crushed more petals in both of his fists and rubbed the petals into the skin of her thighs, pushing her legs farther apart until he could reach her core. He pushed his finger into her body and drew out some of her moisture. He lifted his head to look at her.

Her eyes were closed, her head tipped back and her shoulders arched, throwing her breasts, with their berry-hard tips, forward, begging for more attention. Her entire body was a creamy delight accented by the bloodred petals.

He lowered his head again, hungry for more of her. He feasted on her body the way a starving man would, carefully tasting the moist flesh between her legs. He used his teeth, tongue and fingers to bring her to the brink of climax, but held her there, wanting to draw out the moment of completion until she was begging him for it.

Her hands grasped his head as she thrust her hips toward his face. But he pulled away so that she didn't get the contact she craved.

"Kane, please."

At the words he'd been waiting for, he scraped his teeth over her clitoris, and she screamed as her orgasm rocked through her body. He kept his mouth on her until she stopped shuddering and then slid his body along hers.

"Your turn," she said.

He loved the sensuous side of Mary. Loved that she never held anything back in the bedroom.

She took his erection in her hand, touching her finger to the drop of moisture at the tip. She brought her hand to her mouth and licked her finger.

"Untie my legs," she said.

"I like having you open for me."

"I promise you'll like what I'm going to do."

He bent to untie both of her ankles. As soon as she was free, she pushed him back onto the cushions. Kneeling over him, she brought a handful of petals to his erection and stroked them up and down his length. The velvety softness felt incredibly erotic on his skin.

She followed her hand with her tongue, teasing him with alternating quick licks and light touches. She massaged the petals against his sac and lower. With her thumb and forefinger she circled the base of his shaft, while her mouth covered the tip of him and she began to suck.

He arched off the bed, thrusting up into her before he realized what he was doing. The sensations her mouth and hands aroused in him were almost overwhelming. He pulled her from his body, wanting to be inside her when he came.

She straddled his hips, and, using his grip on her own hips, he pulled her down while he pushed his erection into her body.

He thrust harder and harder, trying to get as deep as possible. He pulled her legs forward, forcing them farther apart until she settled even closer to him. She arched her back, thrusting her breasts forward. He captured her nipple in his mouth, sucking on her mercilessly to heighten her response. He thrust harder and felt every nerve in his body tensing. Reaching between their bodies, he touched her in a sensual caress until he felt her body start to tighten around him.

He climaxed in a hot rush, continuing to thrust into her until his body was drained. She collapsed on top of him, laying her head on his chest, and he turned them on their sides, tugging the coverlet over their cooling bodies. He held her lightly in his arms despite his urge to grip her tightly and ensure she was really his. Even though she now wore his engagement ring, he felt something unsettled between them. The feeling in the pit of his stomach said she remained just out of his reach and he hadn't yet found a way to keep her for the rest of their lives.

Ten

Mary was amazed at how quickly Kane meshed their lives together. His job required him to spend at least eight hours a day on the phone and computer, managing investments and talking to his office and clients. She knew that he needed to return to Manhattan, but she had promised to attend the Eastwick ball—an annual charity event at the end of the week—so he'd postponed his trip until the following week.

He always arrived at her house at four in the afternoon and they spent a couple of hours working on the details of her trust. Everything was coming together smoothly under Kane's guidance.

Their relationship was going so well that she was

reluctant to bring up the past and the secrets she kept from him. Even so, she knew it was only a matter of time before she had to tell him.

The phone rang while she waited for Kane one afternoon about a week after their engagement. "Duvall residence."

"Hi, Mary. It's Abby."

Abby Talbot, another member of the Debs Club, had recently lost her mother, Bunny Baldwin. There was a lot of mystery surrounding Bunny's death. Initially, it was presumed she'd died from natural causes, but with investigation it had been ruled suspicious. There was speculation that her gossip column had garnered an enemy or two, possibly one who'd taken extreme measures to prevent Bunny from talking—especially since her secret journals had been stolen, too. Truthfully, though, Bunny's column had never been malicious, and she'd never printed anything that wasn't verifiable.

"Hey, Abby. What's up?"

"I heard something disturbing in town. And you know how I feel about gossip, but I thought you should hear this from a friend." Given her mother's column and the rampant rumors about her death, Abby was sensitive to gossip.

"Maybe you'd better tell me what you heard."

"Did you know that Kane had a mistress?"

Mary blanched. "When?"

"When he was dating his first wife. Apparently

that was the reason for their divorce. I don't know all the details, but Lorette does, and I'm sure she's going to be stopping by your place before long."

Mary felt her throat tighten and her hands get clammy. She should have known that she wouldn't get the chance at real happiness with Kane, that her past and her secrets would haunt her. "Thanks, Abby. It would have been shocking to hear it from Lorette first."

"You're welcome. Friends have to watch each other's backs."

Abby hung up and Mary sat in her grandfather's big chair realizing that everything she'd been working toward since his death was about to come tumbling down around her. How could she have let this happen?

Kane arrived before she'd had time to totally digest what Abby had told her.

"What's the matter?" he asked.

"Uh, our secret is out."

"What secret?"

"That I was your mistress. That I broke up your first marriage. That I'm still not good enough to be a Duvall."

Kane put down his briefcase and crossed the room to her, reaching out to touch her but she flinched away. She didn't want to be comforted. She didn't deserve it.

"Did I really ruin your marriage, Kane?"

He cursed under his breath, leaning against the desk. "No, you didn't."

"Maybe you'd better tell me what really happened. Lorette knows that you had a mistress and thinks that she's the reason your marriage failed."

"You know the details. You know what happened with Victoria. It had nothing to do with you, even though her family did use the knowledge that I'd kept a mistress to try to force me to stay married to her."

She heard the pain in Kane's voice and knew that this wasn't easy for him, either. She put her hand on his thigh, trying to offer him some of the comfort she'd just refused. She didn't want to see him in pain. She didn't want to think of Kane trying to do the right thing by his brother and failing.

"If your cousins are investigating me, then they probably saw the newspaper articles that were written about the dissolution of my marriage. Your name was never mentioned."

"I don't think that's going to matter," she said, wondering if someone knew that *she* had been Kane's mistress. She wondered if Bunny Baldwin had somehow heard that detail and noted it in her private journal, which was said to contain a lot of secret information that never appeared in her column. If that were the case, the thief now knew about Mary's past. The thief could also have found out that Kane was the father of her child, not Jean-Paul. The time for keeping secrets was slipping away. She couldn't delude herself any longer, she needed to tell Kane everything now.

"I say we face this head-on. We'll go speak to Max tomorrow and simply say that I did have a mistress and that you were that woman. Marriage rights all past wrongs."

"Maybe to some people, but my cousins are going to eat up the fact that I was your mistress."

Kane lifted her out of the chair, sat, then pulled her onto his lap. She rested her head on his shoulder, taking solace from the feel of his strong arms around her.

"That was part of the old Mary. Not the new, proper Mary who wouldn't settle for anything but a wedding ring this time around."

"I didn't demand you marry me," she said.

"No, but we'll put that spin on it. I'll put an end to this mistress business."

If only that were her biggest worry. As if sensing her continued anxiety, Kane tipped her head back and said, "Trust me, Mary-Belle. I'll make this right. This was my fault from the beginning by trying to be too many things to too many people."

His words made her ache inside. "It wasn't your fault, Kane."

"Regardless, I'm fixing it."

She knew there was no changing his mind once he made it up. How was she going to tell him the rest of it? That was the real worry that plagued her, tarnishing the happiness she'd found with him.

"Let's get back to work on the Brent Trust," he said. She stood and he went to get his briefcase.

"Why did you pick the name Brent for this charity?" he asked as he settled in a chair, pulling out a sheaf of papers.

"Brent was the name of my son," she said, unable to keep the throaty emotion from her voice. She had so many regrets. For a while, living in Eastwick had been a nice way to escape them, but no longer.

"Do you want to tell me about him?"

"There's little to tell. He was stillborn. I didn't have money for proper prenatal visits, and since I wasn't a French citizen, I wasn't eligible for their medical benefits."

"Didn't your husband provide for you? What kind of man did you marry?"

She took a deep breath. "Jean-Paul and I weren't married."

"He left you while you were pregnant with his child? What kind of a man was he to leave the mother of his child all alone? That's despicable."

Kane stood and paced the room. She could see the anger in each step he took. Her dreams of understanding from Kane about what she'd done died a swift death. He was never going to forgive her for keeping the truth from him.

"No, Kane. I was never married to Jean-Paul. I just said that when you came to Paris to save face. I didn't want you to think that…to realize no one wanted me."

"What the hell are you talking about? *I* wanted you." And he always had. He'd convinced himself that Mary would stay with him once he married Victoria, even though he knew her American sensibility would forbid her from having an affair with a married man. He really had been a jerk back then.

"To be your mistress. You were getting married. Remember that?" she asked.

He didn't want to think about the fact that his choices—no matter how he'd justified them in his own mind—made him directly responsible for what had happened to Mary. *He'd* left her alone. Not Jean-Paul or any other man. Him, Kane Brentwood, the well-respected peer of the realm—a real ass when it came to this woman.

"I'm sorry, Mary. I screwed that up. But I'm planning to make it up to you."

Mary shook her head. "There's enough blame to go around. As I'm sure Channing will point out."

He wasn't going to argue with her. "I'll take care of this. Your cousins might seem big and bad here in Eastwick, but I've done battle with bigger fish."

"Who?" she asked, sounding weary and looking more fragile than he'd seen her since her grandfather's funeral. Sometimes it felt as though a lifetime had passed in the space of a few weeks.

"Victoria's family. They were determined to make me pay for ending our marriage. But there was no way I was staying any longer. I'm getting good at going up against the in-laws."

The blood left her face, and he realized he'd blundered again by saying the wrong thing. Hell, nothing was easy where Mary was concerned, but he knew, no matter how many times he screwed up or said the wrong thing, he wasn't letting her leave this room until she agreed that they were still engaged.

"That's right—you had to deal with all this with the last woman you asked to marry you," she said, looking up at him, her ocean-blue eyes wide with hurt. "What did you do for her, Kane? Did you fill your house with rose petals and seduce her—"

"Nothing. She had the ring from my brother. She announced it to the papers and it was all done."

"Did you want to marry her?" Mary asked. "I've never really been able to forgive that."

He didn't blame her. "I've never wanted any woman the way I want you."

She tipped her head to the side, studying him intently, and he hoped that whatever it was she sought she would find it.

She sighed and paced to the window that overlooked the terrace, putting her hand on the glass and staring out into the garden area. "The easiest thing to do would be to end the engagement. We only said that we were engaged—"

"No, we didn't only say it. I asked you to marry me and you said yes. I'm not letting you change your mind." He crossed the room to stand behind her, placing his hand over hers on the window and twining their fingers together.

He couldn't lose Mary again. These past few weeks had driven home to him how complete she made his life. He liked coming home to her every day, working on the trust with her, having dinner with her and spending the night with her. He liked knowing when he went to bed each night that he'd wake in the morning with Mary in his arms.

"As much as you might like to think so, Kane, you're not the boss of me," she said without looking at him. "I'm a grown woman. No longer the wild child I used to be. And I think it's time I let Channing and Lorette know that."

He wished he was her boss. Life would be much easier if Mary would simply follow his every order. "*The boss of you?* When did I give you the impression that I thought I was?"

"Every time you say something autocratic like 'I'm not letting you change your mind.'"

She pulled her hand out from under his. He knew he was losing this battle. He tried to put his mind to Mary as if she were a financial investment. How would he analyze it and make it work? But Mary wasn't a spreadsheet; she was his obsession, his woman; and it was time she understood that.

"I'm not being autocratic. I'm simply stating the fact that we are getting married." Nothing she could say would change his mind.

"The fact?" she asked.

Her tone let him know she wasn't too pleased

with his handling of this. But he didn't know any other way. "Yes. The first time I handled everything with you the wrong way."

"I don't know about that. We had some good times," she said, and in her voice he heard the memory of the good times they'd shared.

Those memories were of a life that had been half hidden in shadows, and he didn't want that this time. "But we didn't have an open life. We're not hiding anymore. You're my fiancée, and if your cousins don't back off, they'll find out exactly what kind of man they are messing with."

"I don't want you to stay with me because you think I can't fight my own battles."

He wrapped his arm around her waist and pulled her against his body. He lowered his head to rub his jaw against her silky hair. He didn't want to live without her in his life. If that meant taking on her cousins, the town gossips and the ghosts of their past, then he would do it.

"I'm not fighting them for you because I don't think you can win without me. I'm fighting them for you because I want to be your hero."

She turned in his arms, raising her hands to frame his face. "That's the sweetest thing anyone has ever said to me."

He'd take sweet over that anger and fear he'd heard in her voice earlier. In fact, he'd take her any way she'd have him. He loved this stubborn, complicated, sexy woman. And he wasn't going to let her escape again.

The day of the Eastwick Fall Ball Mary woke up alone. Kane had been called to Manhattan for an emergency meeting. They'd fallen into a tentative peace the past few days. She'd convinced him to leave Channing and Lorette to her for now, but only because she'd agreed to start planning their wedding.

A part of her still wasn't convinced that Kane would stay with her. The pattern of her life was one of loss. And she'd never had any relationship that came as close to normal as the one she was in now with Kane.

She'd suggested going to Felicity to have her help plan their wedding, but Kane didn't want to wait too long, saying they could take care of the details themselves. He wanted them to be married in two weeks on the beach in front of his rented house.

Yesterday she'd received an express-mail package containing photos of flowers that he thought she'd like for her bouquet, as well as two original designs for wedding dresses from Kara Morelli—a designer friend of theirs who was quickly becoming the "it" girl for celebrity weddings.

Kara had called Mary yesterday afternoon to discuss the gown that Mary wanted. In the course of the conversation Kara had expressed her happiness that Mary and Kane were finally back together. As

Mary made her way downstairs after her shower, she shook her head, still feeling a little stunned that they *were* together.

"Good morning, Miss Mary. I set your breakfast up on the terrace. Mr. Previn sent over an envelope for you this morning—it's next to your plate."

"Thank you, Carmen."

Mary sat and opened the envelope tentatively. She wasn't sure what he'd be sending her—maybe a formal notice that her behavior still wasn't up to snuff.

She pulled out the papers, reading them as she nibbled on her blueberry muffin. It was a proposal that he thought would keep her cousins off her back for good. This would be a chance to right the wrongs of the past and maybe lay some of the ghosts that haunted her to rest.

He suggested that she write a new edition of the "Duvall Ladies' Etiquette Guide" using what she'd learned from being the ultimate rebel. In fact, that was his recommended title—"The Rebel's Guide to Ladylike Living."

"What's that?"

She glanced up to see Kane striding through the door. "I thought you weren't going to be here until this afternoon."

"I wanted to surprise you," he said. Since their conversation about the engagement and the threat of rumors, Kane had gone out of his way to prove that he wanted to be her hero. "So what's this?"

"A proposal from Max. He's suggesting that I update the 'Duvall Ladies' Etiquette Guide.'"

He leaned down to kiss her thoroughly. "Ah, that's better. I missed you the last few nights. I'd hoped to get here before you got out of bed."

"You just missed me. Thirty minutes earlier and I'd still have been there," she said, realizing she'd missed him more than she wanted to admit.

He pulled out a chair at the table and sat, reaching for the coffee carafe and the empty mug that Carmen had left on the table. She must have known Kane was coming home and set out the extra dishes.

"I don't suppose I can convince you that you need a nap?" he asked, arching one eyebrow. "The ball tonight will go late."

"A nap at nine in the morning?" Though she wouldn't mind going back to bed with Kane.

"I guess not."

He sounded so disappointed she couldn't help but smile at him. "I might be sleepy this afternoon."

"I'm sure I will be. I stayed up all night finalizing the paperwork for your trust. By the end of the month you should be able to start looking for office space and hiring your staff."

She was touched at how he'd made the trust a priority. Without his help she knew she'd still be trying to figure out which steps to take first.

"I'm not sure where to start the hiring process. I'm

on the board of trustees for the Eastwick Art Council, but that's mostly a local group."

"I've got a few contacts who are experts in developing and running successful charitable trusts," Kane said, handing her a folder that was a quarter of an inch thick. "According to everyone I spoke to, you'll need at least eight people on staff. You'll also need a first-rate Web designer to create the site for the foundation and give people a place to register for the services."

Kane's investment strategy had made it possible for Mary to make the Brent Trust a twofold operation—one that would endow hospitals with neonatal wings and a second separate operation for low-income mothers to apply for money to help pay for prenatal care.

"Thank you so much for all the work you put into this."

"It was nothing," he said.

But she knew it had been something. And more important to her than he probably realized. Or maybe he did realize the importance of this trust and that was why he'd worked so hard to make it come together.

"It is everything, Kane. You took my dreams to help others and made it a reality. I can't thank you enough."

"I didn't do it for thanks, Mary-Belle," he said, taking her hand in his and meshing their fingers together.

No, he'd done it for her. Because he cared about her. She knew that he was still trying to make amends for the past, but there were no further reparations to be made. In the face of his sincerity, her secret felt cold and dark—dirty as it lay in her mind. She needed to tell him he'd been Brent's father. Needed to get that out in the open. But this morning, with the sun shining down on them, she didn't want to say anything.

She stared at Kane for a long time, watching him as he read over Max's proposal and made notes in the margin. Her heartbeat sped up as she acknowledged how much she loved Kane. She'd never really stopped loving him. No matter what happened in the future—if her cousins succeeded in driving a wedge between them, and they had to live their lives apart—she'd always love him.

Eleven

Kane's cell phone rang while they were walking on the beach later that afternoon. "I've got to take this."

"No problem. You don't have to entertain me every second of the day."

"I want to," he said.

"Take your call and then we can talk."

He answered the phone, and Mary moved a few feet away to give him privacy. He wrapped up the conversation quickly, then came up behind her, resting his hands on her shoulders as they stared toward the ocean.

"I'm going to have to participate in a conference call in about ten minutes. Can I use the phone in your study?"

"Yes. I guess it's a good thing we didn't take a nap," she teased.

"As much as I hate to admit it, you're right."

At the house, Mary left Kane to his conference call and went to her studio. She wasn't sure how to tell Kane the truth about Brent. Every time she started to, she stopped.

Her motives were selfish. For the first time in her life she actually felt accepted for who she really was. She wasn't playing a role—the rebel for her family or the sexy mistress for Kane or even the bohemian artist for herself—to get that acceptance. Regardless of how she acted, Kane stood by her.

She was actually making peace with the strictures her grandfather's will had put on her. It was as if, dammit, she was finally growing up. The process wasn't as painful as she'd always thought it would be.

Still, she did have to confess the one lie that lingered between her and Kane—the one thing that was keeping her from fully embracing their relationship.

She locked the door behind her and quickly changed into her painting clothes. She moved her easel into the center of the room, where she had good light from the sun and the overhead track lighting.

Kane's portrait had started out featuring only him. Working on it had given her a chance to explore the new lines on his face that age and life had put there, to reacquaint herself with his familiar looks.

But then almost without conscious thought she'd added herself to the picture, placing herself securely in his arms.

Now, as she dwelled on how to tell Kane about his son, she toyed with the idea of adding Brent to the picture, transferring the mental image of his sweet, peaceful face onto canvas.

It would be the easiest way for her to tell Kane. Words were always a struggle for her when her emotions were involved.

She started painting Brent into the portrait.

As the image emerged, she recognized the elements of the family she'd always craved—loving husband and wife, cherished child. With Kane she finally had an opportunity to see her dream realized. Hope surged through her at the prospect.

For almost two hours she worked, until a knock on the door brought her back to this world.

"Who is it?"

"Kane."

She hurriedly moved her easel so that the canvas wasn't visible from the doorway before opening the door.

"You're painting," he said, rubbing his finger over her cheek. When he lifted his hand she saw a smudge of cerulean on his finger.

"I'm...well, I'm working on a private piece right now. But I have a commission to do a new series similar to my Paris pieces that I need to start soon."

"Can I have a preview?" he asked, tucking her under his shoulder as he walked into the room.

She halted, taking both of his hands in hers, wondering if this would be the moment when the truth just spilled out. It was unexpected, but many of the moments that defined her life were.

"This painting isn't like my normal work, and I'm not sure about it."

"I'm sure it's fabulous like all of your other pieces. Has anyone seen it yet?"

"No. No one here in Eastwick knows that I'm Maribel D."

"How can you keep something like that a secret? Especially now that you are gaining recognition."

"It's a very personal part of me, Kane. I don't want the artist and the Duvall heiress to be linked in public."

"I'm glad to be one of the few you trust with your secrets," he said, his words a double-edged sword. He cupped her face, kissing her lingeringly. "So can I see what you've worked on?"

She shook her head, letting the opportunity to confess pass again. "Not yet. But soon I'll show it to you."

"I can hardly wait."

Now that she'd decided to use her art to share her secret she wanted every detail of the painting to be perfect. She needed to make sure that Kane saw their son as he'd been in her eyes—beautiful, sweet and far too fragile. She shuddered as she remembered holding his tiny body.

Kane pulled her into his arms, stroking her back. "You okay?"

She rested her head against his chest, letting him surround her. She didn't want to respond. She only wanted to close her eyes and pretend that Kane would always want to hold her, that once she made her confession he wouldn't loathe her. Unfortunately reality would not recede. She knew from the way he'd reacted to the news that Jean-Paul had left her alone to give birth to her baby that Kane wasn't going to forgive easily.

She wished now that she hadn't acted in anger on that long-ago day when she'd first lied to Kane. Ironic that she wished now that she'd behaved the way Grandfather had urged her to. Because if she'd counted to ten a few thousand times and kept her temper, she and Kane might have a different history. There might not be so many wasted years between them.

Kane had hired a limo and driver for the evening. Sitting in the back of the car, Mary watched him fiddle with his tie, which was, of course, perfectly knotted.

"What are you doing?" she asked.

"Are you sure a dinner jacket is going to be fine?"

"Yes. You look dashing…like 007."

"Double-oh seven?"

Mary waggled her eyebrows at him. "Don't I look like a Bond girl?"

He caught her by the back of the neck, drawing her closer to him and taking her mouth with his. He didn't pull back until she was leaning against him and holding onto his shoulders for support.

Mary had spent a little more time on her painting before they'd left for the evening and knew that it was ready. Tonight was the night. When they returned home, she'd take him up to her studio to show him the truth of the past. Afterward, they could work out how to have a future together. Having made the decision to tell him, she felt lighter, as if the weight of guilt had left her.

"Come on, Bond girl, we don't want to be any later than we already are."

The chauffeur opened the door and they both exited the car. Kane put his hand on the small of her back—half of his palm rested on the fabric of her evening dress, the other half on the bare skin of her back. He stroked his forefinger gently over her flesh, and she felt a shiver of sensual awareness start deep inside her.

"Do you have to socialize and work the room or do you want to dance?" Kane asked when they entered the ballroom.

"I definitely want to dance with you, but I think I see Abby over there and I want to talk to her. Would you mind getting me a drink?" After their talk the other day, Mary needed to check with Abby to see if she'd heard anything else.

"Not at all. Do you want a martini?"

"Yes, please. Too bad I can't go with you and have you do that Bond thing—*shaken, not stirred.*"

"You are teasing me, Mary-Belle."

"Yes, I am. I intend to drive you out of your mind tonight."

"You already do," he said, kissing her and then firmly pointing her in the direction of her friend. "Fifteen minutes?"

She nodded. It took a few minutes to get across the crowded room to Abby. She appeared to be without her husband, Luke.

"I thought Luke was going to be here tonight," Mary said, hugging her friend.

"He is. I don't know when he'll show up." Abby sipped her glass of champagne. Abby's husband was gone a lot on business.

"You can hang out with Kane and I until he does."

"Thanks, Mary. Where is Kane?" Abby asked, finishing her drink and signaling one of the waitstaff to collect her empty glass.

"Getting some drinks at the bar. I'm not much of a champagne drinker."

"I am," Abby said, taking another glass from a passing tray.

"I can see that. Listen, I wanted to talk to you alone for a minute."

"About?" Abby asked.

Mary looked around the ballroom. This might not be the best place for the conversation, but she couldn't let this opportunity pass. She took Abby's arm and drew her away from the other people to a quiet corner.

"That rumor about Kane's past that you heard the other day..."

"What about it?"

"I wondered if you knew any more details, possibly from another source."

"I told you everything I heard. Why?"

"With Kane and I being the targets of speculation, I'm worried that maybe your mother found out something about my past that I don't want made public."

"I haven't read anything about you in her diaries, if that helps."

Mary was only partially relieved. Just because there was nothing in Bunny's diary didn't mean that there hadn't been notes on Mary's past in the stolen journal.

"My cousins have found out part of it, which is what you heard. The truth is that *I* was Kane's mistress when we lived in London. He paid for my flat and living expenses plus provided me with an investment portfolio in exchange for—"

Abby put her hand on Mary's arm in a show of support. "You don't have to justify yourself to me. I'm not judging you."

Until that moment Mary hadn't realized how much her friend's respect meant to her. She hadn't acknowledged the depth of her fear that Abby might have read something damning about her and withdrawn her friendship as a result.

"I'm finally figuring out some things about my life that I should have a long time ago," Mary said.

"Because of Kane?"

"I think so." She paused. "You know, there's a part of me that can't believe we're really going to get married."

"I like him," Abby said. "He's made you seem…I don't know, not so sad."

"I didn't realize anyone noticed."

"You just haven't been yourself lately."

"I'm not sure that's a bad thing."

"Your mother never understood you, Mary. You were proper in your own way."

Mary smiled at her friend. As she watched Abby drain her glass, she felt compelled to address her friend's consumption. "You seem to be drinking a lot tonight. Is anything wrong, Abby?"

Her friend snagged a third glass of champagne from a passing waiter. It wasn't like Abby to drink this much, but before Mary could pursue it further, they were interrupted.

"Hello, Mary and Abby. Mind if we join you? You look like a couple of wallflowers hiding out," Delia Forrester said. She was wearing a tight dress that left no doubt to her assets, which, rumor had it, had been enhanced by several plastic surgeries.

Yes, Mary thought. This was a part of Eastwick she could do without. She really wanted to find out if Abby was okay and instead she would be forced to chat it up with Delia and Frank Forrester. She actually liked the seventysomething Frank. He'd been a friend of her grandfather's, and the two men had played golf together once a week.

Delia was almost thirty years Frank's junior. Mary didn't really understand their relationship, but Frank seemed happy with his wife.

Mary wanted to say something catty back to Delia, but Kane arrived then and she decided Delia wasn't worth her time. As he handed Mary a martini glass, he lowered his head to give her a very proprietary kiss. "Miss me, darling?"

"Yes."

"I'm afraid we haven't met your fiancé, Mary," Frank said.

"Frank and Delia Forrester, this is Kane Brentwood. Kane, Frank and Delia."

Kane shook Frank's hand. "Nice to meet you."

"What a sexy accent you have," Delia said. "It's no wonder Mary scooped you up so quickly."

"I'm the one who claimed her," Kane said.

Mary shook her head at him. He was in a good mood tonight. But then, he shone in social settings. Apparently she wasn't the only one who saw his appeal, since Delia had settled her hand on Kane's arm. Mary stepped closer to her fiancé in a distinctly possessive move. Kane arched one eyebrow at her, then wrapped his arm around her waist to accommodate her. Their actions effectively squeezed Delia out.

Mary lifted her martini to clink her glass against Kane's. "To our life together."

They both took a sip of their drinks. She loved the icy perfection of a Grey Goose martini.

"That is so touching. You two are picture-perfect. How did you meet?" Delia asked in that saccharinely sweet way of hers.

"We met in a shop in London," Kane said.

"When was that? Tell us all the juicy details," Delia said.

Mary stared at her for a moment, not sure what to say. "There's nothing juicy to tell."

"I'm sure there is," Delia said, taking a sip of her white wine.

"Frank, I heard you had a medical scare a while back," Abby said, forcing the subject away from Mary and Kane's relationship.

"He did, right about the time your mother died, Abby," Delia said.

Mary mouthed a *thank-you* to her friend when Delia turned away. Abby just lifted her champagne flute and took another sip.

"It's kind of strange actually," Frank said. "I'd mixed up my morning and evening medication. Ended up double dosing on my heart medicine. I was lucky to get to the hospital in time."

"Such a close call must have frightened you both," Mary said.

Delia pressed a kiss to her husband's cheek. "It certainly did. We've hired a nurse to make sure that doesn't happen again."

The band returned from their break, playing a cover of "We Are Family." Abby and Mary looked at each other and smiled. "Come on, Kane. This is our song."

"I thought our song was 'Let's Get It On.'"

"I meant this is the Debs' song. We always meet in the middle of the dance floor when it comes on."

"Excuse us, Frank and Delia, my lady wants to dance. It was nice meeting you both."

Mary followed Abby onto the dance floor, keeping hold of Kane's arm. Felicity Farnsworth, Emma Dearborn, Lily Cartwright and Vanessa Thorpe joined them, some with their men in tow some without. They laughed and danced together, enjoying their ritual. Kane disappeared for a few moments but returned before the song ended.

The tempo changed to a slower beat, and Kane drew her into his arms as the first notes of "Let's Stay Together," the classic Al Green song that Tina Turner had made popular, started.

"Did you request this song?" she asked.

"Yes, they didn't know 'Let's Get It On.'"

She wrapped her arms around his shoulders as he led her around the dance floor. His entire body caressed hers as the lead singer's voice played over them. The words of the song took on special resonance as she recognized how aptly they applied to her and Kane.

She reached up to frame his face in her hands and kissed him with all the love and passion that she felt. He held her with the kind of possessiveness that made her feel that there was nothing they couldn't overcome together.

Twelve

Dancing with Mary turned Kane on. And he knew it affected Mary, as well. When the band took another break, he led her off the dance floor. "Ready to go home?"

"Yes, but I want to check on Abby before we leave."

Kane searched for Abby over the crowd and was surprised to find her in the embrace of a man. "I think her husband arrived."

"Really? Where? I can't see over the crowd the way you can."

Kane maneuvered them around until Mary could see her friend from a distance. "Okay. Then I'm ready to go."

"Excellent."

"You sound…"

"Excited?"

"Tired. I think we'll have to go straight to bed."

He laughed at her. "We are definitely going straight to bed. You've kept me waiting all day, and time's up."

He put a protective arm around her waist as they moved through the throng to the exit. While they were waiting for the limo, Emma and her husband, Garrett Keating joined them.

"Did you notice that Luke showed up?" Mary asked.

"Yes. Just in time, if you ask me," Emma replied.

"Just in time for what?"

"Someone poisoned Abby's champagne."

"What? How did she know there was poison in her drink?" Mary was stunned.

"I'm not sure. I think Luke could tell by the scent that it was tainted and stopped her from drinking it."

"Was it deliberate?"

"How could it be?" Kane asked. "All the waiters had trays of champagne."

"I don't think anyone really knows who the target was," Garrett added.

"Well, the rumor mill will be busy tomorrow with speculation," Mary said. She wondered if the attempted poisoning was linked to Bunny's death and the missing journal.

Before she could voice her theory, their limo

arrived. Mary and Emma made plans to visit Abby in the morning to check on her.

"Alone at last," Kane said as the car pulled away from the country club. He drew Mary onto his lap, found her mouth with his and kissed her the way he'd wanted to all night—long, deep and thoroughly. He found the zipper at the side of her dress and lowered it.

"Not quite alone," Mary said, grabbing his wrist to prevent him from cupping her breast. "There's a driver up front there."

"So?" he asked, tugging at her dress until her arms were trapped and the tops of her breasts revealed.

He lowered his head and dropped tiny nibbling kisses along the border of the fabric. Her nipples tightened and she undulated in his arms. He pulled the fabric lower, revealing the edges of her areolae, brushing his tongue across them.

Her hands came up to his head, holding him to her breasts. She shifted her shoulders and one nipple burst free. He suck her deep into his mouth, holding her still with his hands on her waist.

Only when he had her in his arms did he feel as though she was completely his. The rest of the time she seemed to keep a wall between them.

But as he made love to Mary in the car he knew there were no obstacles between them. They were perfectly compatible. He loved her scent, the womanly smell that was unique to Mary. He loved her taste, the sweet-salty flavor of her skin. He loved her breathy little sighs as her passion built.

Suddenly their car screeched to a halt, throwing them off balance. Kane wrapped his arms around Mary as they both rolled to the floor. He took the impact of the fall, holding her close to him, keeping her safe in his arms.

She pulled the bodice of her dress into place as Kane lifted her back onto the seat. He lowered the partition between them and the driver.

"What happened? Are you okay?" Kane asked the driver. There were lights from another car off the other side of the road.

"A deer jumped out and the car in front of me slammed on the brakes. I'm fine. Are you both okay?"

"Yes," Kane said. "Does the other driver need our assistance?"

"I'll go check. The car spun around when he tried to stop."

"I'll call 911 and get some help," Mary said.

Kane got out with the driver and checked on the other vehicle. Although the other driver appeared unhurt, the ambulance arrived a few minutes later and the paramedics checked him over. A police officer arrived on scene, as well, to take everyone's statements.

Once they were back in the limo, Kane raised the partition. He held Mary close. "Are you okay?"

"I'm fine. How about you? You took the weight of our fall."

"Are you sure?" He ignored her query as he ran his hands over her arms and back. He didn't like the thought that she could be hurt.

"Yes, Kane, I'm fine. What about you?"

"That doesn't matter."

"Did you get hurt?"

"No."

She cuddled close to his side. "Thank you for being my hero."

Carmen was waiting for them when they got home. "You had a call, Mr. Brentwood. The caller said it was urgent."

"Thank you, Carmen," he said, accepting the paper with a phone number on it from her. He'd been expecting to hear from Bill Hutchins regarding the job offer Kane had made him the last time they'd spoken. Even though it was eleven o'clock here, it would only be about eight on the west coast, so Kane could still return the call.

"Why don't you use the study, Kane?" Mary suggested. "I'll put together a nightcap for us on the terrace."

"I'd rather you put together something for us—"

"Kane." She interrupted him by putting her fingers over his lips. A faint blush covered her cheeks, and he knew she was conscious of Carmen's awareness of their intimate lives.

He squeezed Mary's hand. "That sounds wonderful. I'll meet you on the terrace."

He heard Carmen asking about the ball as he closed the door to the study. Since he'd started using Mary's office for business calls, he'd installed one of his company phones that had a digital-recording feature that they used to record all investment calls. It was a safeguard that Kane used against investors' selective memories when stocks didn't perform the way they'd expected.

He'd use that feature tonight so that he'd have an accounting of everything that he and Bill negotiated in terms of employment and benefits.

He dialed the phone, frowning when he didn't recognize the number at Bill's. Maybe it was a cell phone. When the call connected he said. "This is Kane Brentwood."

"Are you alone?" a voice asked. It sounded like a woman, but he couldn't place the voice.

That this call wasn't from Bill was a disappointment. He wanted to wrap this up quickly so he could get back to Mary and his plans for the rest of this night.

"Yes. Who is this?" Kane asked, ready to hang up.

"A concerned friend," the woman replied.

"Why concerned?" Kane asked, trying to identify the speaker. Was it Victoria? The last time they'd talked she'd been livid about Mary.

"Because Mary is a dangerous woman."

"Victoria?"

"No, I'm not your ex-wife."

This was ridiculous. "I'm not interested in hearing this kind of garbage."

"Did you know that she has a secret? One that affects you?"

"What are you talking about?" As much as he wanted to, Kane couldn't bring himself to end the call just yet.

"I think you'd be interested to know that Mary has never been married before."

"That's hardly cause for concern." Kane couldn't believe this person had dug into Mary's past and clearly thought that Mary hadn't confided in him. He was surprised this person hadn't discovered that he'd kept Mary as his mistress for years before her relationship with Jean-Paul.

"She was pregnant in Paris. An unwed mother."

"This is a complete waste of my time."

"Ask Mary who the father of her baby is."

Kane hesitated. "Why?"

"Just do it;" the woman said before hanging up.

He returned the phone to the cradle, then sat back in the leather chair. Had Mary been involved with a third man? He didn't think it was possible.

He checked that the digital recording was saved and then went to find Mary. He paused in the doorway leading to the terrace. A bucket of ice with a bottle of champagne chilling in it sat in the middle of the table. There were two champagne flutes next to the bucket.

Mary was standing beside her easel a short distance away. The torches around the edge of the patio had been lit, and the pool and landscape lighting was on. The moonlight contributed ambience to the area.

The scene was at odds with the conversation he'd just had. Whoever had called him had done so in an attempt to hurt this woman. The woman whom he had vowed to protect from being harmed again—by him or by anyone else.

She lifted the canvas from the chair where she'd rested it and set it on the easel.

"Is this a private showing?"

She turned around quickly, a tentative smile on her face. "Yes. Just for you. Did Bill accept your employment offer?"

"The call wasn't from Bill."

"Who was it from?" she asked, nervously adjusting the fabric that covered the canvas.

"I don't know. Some woman who warned me about you," he said, leaning against the wall and watching her.

"What? What did she say?" she asked.

"She wanted me to believe you'd had secrets you'd do anything to keep quiet."

Mary didn't respond. With each passing moment he felt an inexplicable anxiety rise in him, which was crazy given that she was the victim.

"You said it was a woman who told you this," Mary said finally, not addressing his comment about her secrets.

"Yes," Kane said, crossing the terrace to stand next to her.

"I wonder who it could be. Did you recognize the voice?"

"No, but I did record the call. We can both listen to it later."

"Why later?"

"She told me to ask you something, Mary."

"What?"

"Who is the father of your child?"

All of the color washed out of Mary's face and she reached behind her to grab the chair for support. At her response, Kane's anxiety launched into full-scale dread. This couldn't be good.

Mary felt her knees collapse, but Kane was there before she could fall. She wanted to rest against him, to let his strong arms wrap around her and keep the world at bay. But she'd waited too long in silence and the time for accepting his comfort had passed.

Who was Kane's mystery caller and where had she gotten her information? Was she the thief—and perhaps Bunny's murderer—who had stolen Bunny's private journal? Or had the thief spread the information and the caller was trying to create mayhem? It was possible that none of this was related to Bunny, that the caller had discovered Mary's secret some other way.

"I think I need to sit down," she said, pulling away

from Kane to sit on one of the Adirondack chairs. Kane took a seat in the one next to her.

"Are you going to answer me?"

"Yes. I'd been planning to talk to you about that very subject tonight."

"Really? Why?"

"Because I never slept with Jean-Paul. I tried to tell you the night you asked me to marry you. I wanted to get this out in the open before we started a new life together."

"There was another man, though. Someone else you were involved with."

She took a deep breath. He was angry at the thought of her being with another man, but she knew that he wouldn't be relieved when she told him there hadn't been anyone else. She was a little afraid of how he'd react. Afraid that he would walk out of her life. But there was no more hiding.

"No, Kane. There's never been any other man for me except you."

"But then that means…"

"You were the father of my child."

He said nothing but sank back in the chair, closing his eyes.

"I received two pieces of news the day I left London. The first from my doctor telling me I was pregnant. The second…well, that came from the newspaper telling me that the father of my child was engaged to another woman."

Kane opened his eyes, looking at her with emotions that she really couldn't read. She swallowed hard and forced herself to go on. "I didn't know what to do. I knew I couldn't stay only to see you marry someone else, so I fled to Paris and Jean-Paul. He offered me a place to stay."

"Why didn't you tell me this when I tracked you down?" Kane demanded, his tone harsh and irate.

"I almost did. But then you asked me to be your mistress. Do you remember that, Kane? You asked me to live in that same luxurious flat, where I'd had you all to myself, and be your second—your hidden—life. I couldn't do that to a child. I couldn't accept that for us. And I think I knew even then that you wouldn't abandon your own child."

"So you made up a lie. You took my child from me, Mary," Kane said. "All this time you've kept this knowledge from me. You let me try to make amends for Victoria when this big lie lay between us."

Mary shook her head. "I paid for that. I'm still paying for it."

"Tell me all of it. How did our child die?"

"I didn't have any money in Paris. You'd put a hold on all my accounts and I was cut off from my family. Jean-Paul was kind enough to give me a place to stay, but I couldn't take money from him, as well. So I didn't have regular doctor's visits."

Mary stood, unable to stay seated while she talked about that period of her life. It was at once the best time of her life because she'd wanted to be a mother and the worst because she'd felt so alone and so afraid that her decisions weren't the right ones. "I started working in Jean-Paul's gallery and saved my money to hire a midwife to attend the birth."

"The labor was long and intense, and when the baby was born the umbilical cord was wrapped around his neck. He died during the labor. Even with proper prenatal care, there was little that could have saved him."

She wrapped her arms around her waist, holding herself tightly to contain the emotions that were straining to get free. She wanted to rant at Kane, but she knew that the blame for Brent's death lay on her shoulders. She'd lied to Kane to try to hurt him, and the backlash had hurt her.

"I was devastated. I can't begin to tell you what it was like to be so close to having a family of my own only to have it taken away so quickly—"

"Actually I can understand that. It's the same thing you've done to me by lying about your pregnancy. You stole my chance at those dreams, Mary."

"Be honest, Kane. You wouldn't have left Victoria for me and our child."

Kane stalked over to her. "Neither of us knows what I would have done."

She knew then that revenge ran both ways. In trying to cause him pain, she'd pained herself. There was nothing she could say to make it up to him. She saw the sadness in his eyes and knew he was mourning their child.

"I'm so sorry. If I'd been less stubborn, maybe we'd have our child today. But I couldn't ask you for help, not after you'd left."

"I can't accept your apology. This goes beyond a simple *I'm sorry.*"

"I know, Kane. I think I've known it from the very beginning. That's why I put off telling you for so long," she said through the tears streaming down her face. "I know there's nothing left to say between us."

Mary left the terrace and went into the cold, empty house. Secure in the knowledge that she'd spend the rest of her life here…alone.

Thirteen

Kane watched Mary leave but didn't follow her. He needed time alone away from her. He walked through the garden down to the beach. With the wind blowing in from the water, he sank to the sand.

He'd had a son. When Mary had told him of her little boy, he'd felt sadness because the boy's death had obviously hurt her. But now the pain was sharper because it was *his* son. Tears burned the backs of his eyes and he pushed the heels of his hands against his eyes until the burning stopped.

He pushed to his feet and started walking, his mind focused on the past—a past he couldn't change. He hated the feeling of impotence that came with that knowledge. When he came to the beach entrance of his house he went inside.

It was cold, quiet, empty. He should return to Manhattan, where he'd at least have the noise of the city to fill the background and provide the illusion that he wasn't alone.

He went to the liquor cabinet and found the bottle of single malt scotch that he kept in the back. He poured himself a glass and tossed it back quickly. It stung as it went down, and Kane refilled his glass, then took the bottle and glass with him to sit.

He remembered the night Mary had come here and drunk too much. Remembered the shadows in her eyes and understood for the first time what she'd been battling. Hell, she'd been living with the fact that their son had died for three long years. She'd also been living with the fact that her lover didn't care enough to pay attention to details he should have.

He put the bottle on the floor beside him and thought about all he knew of Mary. She'd been battered by their relationship the same way he had and she hadn't trusted him. She hadn't trusted him enough to tell him they'd had a son together. He could only blame himself because he hadn't given her much to trust in.

Kane rubbed the back of his neck. He didn't want to go back to the life he'd had without Mary. The past few weeks had been the best of his life. And he needed Mary...he'd always known that even if he didn't always admit it. He wasn't about to let her slip away again.

They belonged together in a way Kane couldn't explain. He stood up, glancing at the clock and realizing several hours had passed. It was nearing sunrise. He wanted to go to Mary right now and hash things out with her. He wanted her to understand that they weren't going to spend the rest of their lives apart.

He went to his bedroom to shower and change and then retraced his steps along the beach to her house. Someone had moved the canvas and easel into the living room, Kane noticed as he entered the house from the terrace door.

He removed the fabric to look at the painting Mary had been working on so hard. His breath caught in his chest. He now knew what his son looked like.

Tears burned his eyes again and this time he didn't wipe them away. He let them fall for the family that might have been. He vowed that he and Mary would have more children, that their dream of a family would come true.

The doorbell rang, the chimes echoing through the quiet house. Kane went to answer and encountered Mary at the bottom of the stairs. She looked tired, as if she hadn't gotten any more sleep last night than he had. He wanted to take her in his arms and hold her, tell her that he was sorry for the way he'd acted.

"I didn't realize you were still here," she said.

"I just came back. We have to talk."

The doorbell rang again.

"Where's Carmen?" he asked.

"She doesn't get here until eight."

Kane crossed the foyer and opened the door, wanting to deal quickly with whoever was there so he could then get everything settled with Mary.

Channing and Lorette stood on the doorstep. "A little early for a social call, isn't it?" Kane asked.

"We're here about a legal matter," Channing said, trying to push past Kane into the house.

Kane didn't budge.

"Don't mess with me, Brentwood. You have no idea the trouble I can cause you. I know all your dirty little secrets."

"I doubt that, Moorehead."

"Mary, let us in. You're going to want to hear what we've found out about this man," Lorette said.

Mary came up behind him. Putting her hand on his where he held the door, she slowly peeled his fingers away. "Let them in, please."

Kane did as she asked, stepping out of the way to let them pass. He barely resisted the urge to trip Channing as he entered the foyer.

Kane closed the door. "We can do this here. No use in both of you getting comfortable."

"Why not? Once we go see Max, this house and the entire Duvall fortune will be ours."

"Just get to the good part," Kane said.

"Yes, the good part. Well, it seems that Kane's

lover had his child. Did you know that, Mary?" Channing's smug voice grated on Kane.

Mary went completely white. "Yes, I knew that."

Lorette stepped closer to Mary, her eyes narrowing on her cousin. Kane placed himself between the two women to prevent contact between them. "That's it. That's the big news you've uncovered? You should know Mary isn't responsible for my actions."

"Yes, she is. *She* was your mistress. We know all about it. And that kind of behavior doesn't fit with the stipulations of Uncle David's will," Lorette declared.

"No wonder Mary told me she had no family when we met in London. You people don't know the first thing of what it means to care about someone."

"That doesn't change the fact that once word gets out about you and Mary, the inheritance will come to us," Channing boasted.

"You're not going to say a word about Mary or me to anyone."

"Why not?"

"If you do, I'll ruin you financially. I'm not bluffing. If you've spent as much time digging into my background as it appears you have, you know I can do it."

"Why would you do that? You didn't care enough for Mary to stay with her when she was pregnant with your child."

"You know nothing about my feelings for Mary. You can leave. I'll contact Max this morning for full disclosure. We're not hiding the facts of our past from anyone. There's no scandal where there is truth." Kane opened the front door. "Now get out."

Channing and Lorette left without another word. Kane turned to face Mary, only to find himself alone in the foyer. Before he went to find her, he needed to call her attorney and make sure that her cousins couldn't do any damage to Mary or the funds she wanted to use to set up her charitable trust.

Mary went outside to the gardens beyond the pool and sat on a bench. She'd left when Lorette had said that Kane didn't care about her or their child. She couldn't bring herself to listen to Kane's blunt response. He wasn't a man to lie—even to spare her feelings—and she knew the truth of his commitment to her.

It had been plain last night that love was the last emotion he felt for her. Loving him was a dull ache because she knew that he wasn't about to forgive her, wasn't going to suddenly realize he couldn't live without her. She'd spent the night tossing and turning, trying to think of some way for the two of them to have a relationship.

She'd tried to imagine what she could say to change his mind. To convince him that once she'd made up her stubborn mind about keeping her pregnancy secret, it had been too late to change it. Her pride and her humiliation at being the other woman had kept her silent.

She'd made a real mess of her life, a mess that

she'd finally figured out how to straighten up. But it was too late for her and Kane.

"Mary?" Kane called her name from somewhere near the pool.

She almost didn't answer. If she didn't talk to him this morning, maybe she could find a way around the obstacles between them. But she was through running, she reminded herself.

"Over here."

He came up the path a few moments later. He looked tired as he approached her. She wrapped her arms around her waist, holding herself so that she wouldn't reach out to touch his face and smooth the lines around his eyes and mouth.

He walked right up to the bench and went down on one knee in front of her.

"What are you doing?"

"Asking you to forgive me. Until I heard your cousin's words I didn't realize how you must have felt when I left you for Victoria. I didn't understand how the world would see you and I until that moment. I can't bear the thought that I hurt you that way when all I've ever wanted to do is protect you."

"You can't protect me from the past, Kane. We both made choices that led to—"

He sat on the bench beside her and took her hands in his. "We can't undo the past. But we can make our future a better one."

"What future?" she asked. "I can't live with you

if you don't love me. I was willing to give it a try, but last night I realized that I was still settling for less than what I need from you."

"I don't want you to settle. We need each other, Mary-Belle. We always have. From the moment we met I told myself you were an obsession. That time would dull the sharp ache I had for you."

"Did it?"

"No. Never. From the moment I first made love to you I felt wrapped up in your affection. I know your family wasn't the loving kind, yet you always showered affection on everyone who came into your life. I lived for the hours I spent in your arms in that flat. And yet I almost regret that time together."

She tugged her hands free of his, not sure she could believe him. But Kane had never lied to her. Not once. Even when it would have been in his best interest to do so, he'd stuck to the truth.

"What are you trying to say?"

"That I wish I could go back to when we met in Harrods and do things differently…properly."

"Why?"

"Because I knew from that moment that—"

He pulled her into his arms, holding her so tightly she could barely breathe. His lips brushed her ear, and she felt his mouth move, but she couldn't hear what he said.

She leaned away and looked into his dark eyes. "What did you say?"

He shook his head. "I—I love you, Mary Duvall. I can't imagine living without you. I shouldn't have wasted a moment of our lives together by making you my mistress. I should have asked you to be my wife."

Her breath stopped for a second, then she framed his face with her hands and kissed him softly. "I love you, too."

Kane lifted her into his arms and started walking to the house.

"Where are you taking me?"

"To bed. I want to make love to you and then spend the day talking about our future together."

* * * * *

Don't miss the exciting conclusion of the
SECRET LIVES OF SOCIETY WIVES.
Look for THE PART-TIME WIFE
By Maureen Child
Coming in October 2006
from Silhouette Desire.

Set in darkness beyond the ordinary world.
Passionate tales of life and death.
With characters' lives ruled by laws the everyday world can't begin to imagine.

Introducing NOCTURNE, *a spine-tingling new line from Silhouette Books.*

The thrills and chills begin with UNFORGIVEN by Lindsay McKenna.

Plucked from the depths of hell, former military sharpshooter Reno Manchahi was hired by the government to kill a thief, but he had a mission of his own. Descended from a family of shape-shifters, Reno vowed to get the revenge he'd thirsted for all these years. But his mission went awry when his target turned out to be a powerful seductress, Magdalena Calen Hernandez, who risked everything to battle a potent evil. Suddenly, Reno had to transform himself into a true hero and fight the enemy that threatened them all. He had to become a Warrior for the Light….

Turn the page for a sneak preview of UNFORGIVEN by Lindsay McKenna.
On sale September 26,
wherever books are sold.

Chapter 1

One shot...one kill.

The sixteen-pound sledgehammer came down with such fierce power that the granite boulder shattered instantly. A spray of glittering mica exploded into the air and sparkled momentarily around the man who wielded the tool as if it were a weapon. Sweat ran in rivulets down Reno Manchahi's drawn, intense face. Naked from the waist up, the hot July sun beating down on his back, he hefted the sledgehammer skyward once more. Muscles in his thick forearms leaped and biceps bulged. Even his breath was focused on the boulder. In his mind's eye, he pictured Army General Robert Hampton's fleshy, arrogant fifty-year-old features on the rock's surface. Air exploded from between his lips as he brought the avenging hammer down. The boulder pulverized beneath his funneled hatred.

One shot...one kill...

Nostrils flaring, he inhaled the dank, humid heat and drew it deep into his massive lungs. Revenge allowed Reno to endure his imprisonment at a U.S. Navy brig near San Diego, California. Drops of sweat were flung in all directions as the crack of his sledgehammer claimed a third stone victim. Mouth taut, Reno moved to the next boulder.

The other prisoners in the stone yard gave him a wide berth. They always did. They instinctively felt his simmering hatred, the palpable revenge in his cinnamon-colored eyes, was more than skin-deep.

And they whispered he was different.

Reno enjoyed being a loner for good reason. He came from a medicine family of shape-shifters. But even this secret power had not protected him—or his family. His wife, Ilona, and his three-year-old daughter, Sarah, were dead. Murdered by Army General Hampton in their former home on USMC base in Camp Pendleton, California. Bitterness thrummed through Reno as he savagely pushed the toe of his scarred leather boot against several smaller pieces of gray granite that were in his way.

The sun beat down upon Manchahi's naked shoulders, grown dark red over time, shouting his half-Apache heritage. With his straight black hair grazing his thick shoulders, copper skin and broad face with high cheekbones, everyone knew he was Indian. When he'd first arrived at the brig, some of the prisoners taunted him and called him Geronimo. Something strange happened to Reno during his fight with the name-calling prisoners. Leaning down after he'd won the scuffle, he'd snarled into each of their bloodied faces that if they were going to call him anything, they would call him *gan,* which was the Apache word for *devil.*

His attackers had been shocked by the wounds on their faces, the deep claw marks. Reno recalled doubling his fist as they'd attacked him en masse. In that split second, he'd gone into an altered state of consciousness. In times of danger, he transformed into a jaguar. A deep, growling sound had emitted from his throat as he defended himself in the three-against-one fracas. It all happened so fast that he thought he had imagined it. He'd seen his hands morph into a forearm and paw, claws extended. The slashes left on the three men's faces after the fight told him he'd begun to shape-shift. A fist made bruises and swelling; not four perfect, deep claw marks. Stunned and anxious, he hid the knowledge of what else he was from these prisoners. Reno's only defense was to make all the prisoners so damned scared of him and remain a loner.

Alone. Yeah, he was alone, all right. The steel hammer swept downward with hellish ferocity. As the granite groaned in protest, Reno shut his eyes for just a moment. Sweat dripped off his nose and square chin.

Straightening, he wiped his furrowed, wet brow and looked into the pale blue sky. What got his attention was the startling cry of a red-tailed hawk as it flew over the brig yard. Squinting, he watched the bird. Reno could make out the rust-colored tail on the hawk. As a kid growing up on the Apache reservation in Arizona, Reno knew that all animals that appeared before him were messengers.

Brother, what message do you bring me? Reno knew one had to ask in order to receive. Allowing the sledgehammer to drop to his side, he concentrated on the hawk who wheeled in tightening circles above him.

Freedom! the hawk cried in return.

Reno shook his head, his black hair moving against his broad, thickset shoulders. *Freedom? No way, Brother. No way.* Figuring that he was making up the hawk's shrill message, Reno turned away. Back to his rocks. Back to picturing Hampton's smug face.

Freedom!

* * * * *